THE TRANSFORMATION OF
MISS MAVIS MING

Born in London in 1939, Michael Moorcock has been a professional writer and editor since the age of fifteen, as well as a professional guitarist/singer until the early sixties. He has written novels, thrillers, comedy, poetry, criticism and science fiction. In 1966 the British Science Fiction Award was given to *New Worlds*, of which he became editor in 1964. He has also received the Nebula Award (for *Behold the Man*), the British Fantasy Award (for *Knight of the Swords*) and the August Derleth Award. He has two daughters and a son and lives in London.

THE
TRANSFORMATION OF
MISS MAVIS MING

A Romance of the End of Time
by
Michael Moorcock

A STAR BOOK
published by
the Paperback Division of
W. H. ALLEN & Co. Ltd

A Star Book
Published in 1980
by the Paperback Division of
W. H. Allen & Co. Ltd
A Howard and Wyndham Company
44 Hill Street, London W1X 8LB

First published in Great Britain by
W. H. Allen & Co. Ltd.

Copyright © 1977 by Michael Moorcock

Printed in Great Britain by
Richard Clay (The Chaucer Press) Ltd, Bungay, Suffolk

ISBN 0 352 30649 1

A little something for Alfie Bester

Kindle me to constant fire,
Lest the nail be but a nail!
Give me wings of great desire,
Lest I look within and fail!

... Red of heat to white of heat,
Roll we to the Godhead's feet!
Beat, beat! white of heat,
Red of heat, beat, beat!

—George Meredith
The Song of Theodolinda.

CHAPTER ONE

*In which your Auditor gives Credit to
his Sources*

The incidents involving Mr Jherek Carnelian and Mrs Amelia Underwood, their adventures in Time, the machinations of, among others, the Lord of Canaria, are already familiar to those of us who follow avidly any fragment of gossip coming back from the End of Time.

We know, too, why it is impossible to learn further details of how life progresses there since the inception of Lord Jagged's grand (and some think pointless) scheme, details of which have been published in the three volumes jointly entitled *The Dancers at the End of Time* and in the single volume, companion to this, called *Legends from the End of Time*.

Time travellers, of course, still visit the periods immediately preceding the inception of the scheme. They bring us back those scraps of scandal, speculation, probable fact and likely lies which form the bases for the admittedly fanciful reconstructions I choose to term my 'legends from the future'— stories which doubtless would cause much amusement if those I write about were ever to read them (happily, there is no evidence that the tales survive our present century, let alone the next few million years).

If this particular tale seems more outrageous and less likely than any of the others, it is because I was gullible enough to believe the sketch of it I had from an acquaintance who does not normally journey so far into the future. A colleague of Miss Una Persson in the Guild of Temporal Adventurers, he does not wish me to reveal his name and this, fortunately, allows me to be rather more frank about him than would have been possible.

My friend's stories are always interesting, but they are consistently highly-coloured; his exploits have been bizarre and his claims incredible. If he is to be believed, he has been present at a good many of the best-known key events in history, including the crucifixion of Christ, the massacre at Mei Lei, the assassination of Naomi Jacobsen in Paris and so on, and has often played a major role.

From his base in West London (twentieth century, Sectors 3 and 4) my friend has ranged what he terms the 'chrono-flow', visiting periods of the past and future of this Earth as well as those of other Earths which, he would have us accept, co-exist with ours in a complex system of intersecting dimensions making up something called the 'multiverse'.

Of all the temporal adventurers I have known, my friend is the most ready to describe his exploits to anyone who will listen. Presumably, he is not subject to the Morphail Effect (which causes most travellers to exercise the greatest caution regarding their actions and conversations in any of the periods they visit) mainly because few but the simple-minded, and those whose logical faculties have been ruined by drink, drugs or other forms of dissipation, will take him seriously.

My friend's own explanation is that he is not affected by such details; he describes himself rather wildly as a 'Chronic Outlaw' (a self-view which might give the reader some insight into his character). You might think he charmed me into believing the tale he told me of Miss Mavis Ming and Mr Emmanuel Bloom, and yet there is something about the essence of the story that inclined me to believe it—for all that it is, in many ways, one of the most incredible I have heard. It cannot, of course, be verified readily (certainly so far as the final chapters are concerned) but it is supported by other rumours I have heard, as well as my own previous knowledge of Mr Bloom (whose earlier incarnation appeared in a tale, told to me by one of my friend's fellow Guild Members, published variously as *The Fireclown* and *The Winds of Limbo*, some years ago).

10

The events recorded here follow directly upon those recorded in *Legends from the End of Time* and in effect take up Miss Ming's story where we left it after her encounter with Dafnish Armatuce and her son Snuffles.

As usual, the basic events described are as I had them from my source. I have re-arranged certain things, to maintain narrative tensions, and added to an earlier, less complete, draft of my own which was written hastily, before all the information was known to me. The 'fleshing out' of the narrative, the interpretations where they occur, many of the details of conversations, and so on, must be blamed entirely on your auditor.

In the previous volume to this, I have already recounted something of that peculiar relationship existing between Miss Ming and Doctor Volospion: the unbearable bore and that ostentatious misanthrope.

Why Doctor Volospion continued to take perverse pleasure in the woman's miserable company, why she allowed him to insult her in the most profound of ways—she who spent the greater part of her days avoiding any sort of pain—we cannot tell. Suffice to say that relationships of this sort exist in our own society and can be equally puzzling.

Perhaps Doctor Volospion found confirmation of all his misanthropy in her; perhaps she preferred this intense, if unpleasant, attention to no attention at all. She confirmed his view of life, while he confirmed her very existence.

But it is the purpose of a novel, not a romance, to speculate in this way and it is no part of my intention to dwell too much upon such thoughts.

Here, then, for the reader's own interpretation (if one is needed), is the tale of Miss Ming's transformation and the part which both Doctor Volospion and Emmanuel Bloom had in it.

Michael Moorcock,
Ladbroke Grove,
November 1975.

CHAPTER TWO

In which Miss Mavis Ming Experiences a Familiar
Discomfort

The peculiar effect of one sun rising just as another set, causing shadows to waver, making objects appear to shift shape
and position, went more or less entirely unobserved by the
great crowd of people who stood, enjoying a party, in the foot-
hills of a rather poorly-finished range of mountains erected
some little time ago by Werther de Goethe during one of his
periodic phases of attempting to recreate the landscapes, faithful to the last detail, of Holman Hunt, an ancient painter
Werther had discovered in one of the rotting cities.

Werther, it is fair to say, had not been the first to make such
an attempt. However, he held to the creed that an artist should,
so far as his powers allowed, put up everything exactly as he
saw it in the painting. Werther was a purist. Werther volubly
denied the criticisms of those who found such literal work
bereft of what they regarded as true artistic inspiration.
Werther's theories of Fidelity to Art had enjoyed a short-lived
vogue (for a time the Duke of Queens had been an earnest
acolyte) but his fellows had soon tired of such narrow disci-
plines.

Werther, alone, refused to renounce them.

As the party progressed another of the suns eventually
vanished while the other rose rapidly, reached zenith and
stopped. The light became golden, autumnal, misty. Of the
guests but three had paused to observe the phenomenon: they
were Miss Mavis Ming, plump and eager in her new dress; Li
Pao, bland in puritanical denim; and Abu Thaleb, their host,
svelte and opulent, splendidly overdressed.

'Whose suns?' murmured Abu Thaleb appreciatively. 'How pretty! And subtle. Rivals, perhaps . . .'

'To your own creations?' asked Li Pao.

'No, no—to one another.'

'They could be Werther's,' suggested Miss Ming, anxious to return to their interrupted topic. 'He hasn't arrived yet. Go on, Li Pao. You were saying something about Doctor Volospion.'

A fingered ear betrayed Li Pao's embarrassment. 'I spoke of no one specifically, Miss Ming.' His round, Chinese face became expressionless.

'By association,' Abu Thaleb prompted, a somewhat sly smile manifesting itself within his pointed beard, 'you spoke of Volospion.'

'Ah! You would make a gossip of me. I disdain such impulses. I merely observed that only the weak hate weakness; only the wounded condemn the pain of others.' He wiped a stain of juice from his severe blouse and turned his back on the tiny sun.

Miss Ming was arch. 'But you *meant* Doctor Volospion, Li Pao. You were *suggesting* . . .'

A tide of guests flowed by, its noise drowning what remained of her remark, and when it had passed Li Pao (perhaps piqued by an element of truth) chose to show impatience. 'I do not share your obsession with your protector, Miss Ming. I generalised. The thought can scarcely be considered a specific one, nor an original one. I regret it. If you prefer, I retract it.'

'I wasn't *criticising*, Li Pao. I was just *interested* in how you saw him. I mean, he has been very *kind* to me, and I wouldn't like anybody to think I wasn't aware of all he's *done* for me. I could still be in his menagerie couldn't I? But he showed his respect for me by letting me go—that is, asking me to be his *guest* rather than—well, whatever you'd call it.'

'He is a model of chivalry.' Abu Thaleb stroked an eyebrow and hid his face with his hand. 'Well, if you will excuse me, I must see to my monsters. To my guests.' He departed, to be swallowed by his party, while Li Pao's imploring look went unnoticed.

Miss Ming smoothed the front of Li Pao's blouse. 'So you see,' she said, 'I was only curious. It certainly wasn't *gossip* I wanted to hear. But I respect your opinions, Li Pao. We are fellow "prisoners", after all, in this world. Both of us would probably prefer to be back in the past, where we belong—you in the twenty-seventh century, to take your rightful position as chairman or whatever of China, and me in the twenty-first, to, to ...' Inspiration left her momentarily. She contented herself with a coy wink. 'You mustn't pay any attention to little Mavis. There's no malice in her.'

'Aha.' Li Pao closed his eyes and drew a deep breath.

Miss Ming's sky-blue nail traced patterns on the more restrained blue of his chest. 'It's not in Mavis' nature to think naughty thoughts. Well, not that sort of naughty thought, at any rate!' She giggled.

'Yaha?' It was almost inaudible.

From somewhere overhead came the distant strains of one of Abu Thaleb's beasts. Li Pao raised his head as if to seek the source. He contemplated Heaven.

Miss Ming, too, looked up. 'Nothing,' she said. 'It must have come from over there.' She pointed and, to her chagrin, her finger indicated the approaching figure of Ron Ron Ron who was, like herself and Li Pao, an expatriate (although in his case from the 140th century). 'Oh, look out, Li Pao. It's that bore Ron coming over ...'

She was surprised when Li Pao expressed enthusiastic delight. 'My old friend!'

She was sure that Li Pao found Ron Ron Ron just as awful as everyone else but, for his sake, she smiled as sweetly as she could. 'How *nice* to see you!'

Ron Ron Ron had an expression of *hauteur* on his perfectly oval face. This was his usual expression. He, too, seemed just a little surprised by Li Pao's effusion. 'Um?'

The two men contemplated one another. Mavis plainly felt that it was up to her to break the ice. 'Li Pao was just saying— *not* about Doctor Volospion or anybody in particular—that the weak hate weakness and won't—what was it, Li Pao?'

'It was not important, Miss Ming. I must ...' He offered

14

Ron Ron Ron a thin smile.

Ron Ron Ron cleared his throat. 'No, please ...'

'It was very *profound*,' said Miss Ming. 'I thought.'

Ron Ron Ron adjusted his peculiar jerkin so that the edges were exactly in line. He fussed at a button. 'Then you must repeat it for me, Li Pao.' The shoulders of his jerkin were straight-edged and the whole garment was made to the exact proportions of a square. His trousers were identical oblongs; his shoes, too, were exactly square. The fingers of his hands were all of the same length.

'Only the weak hate weakness ...' murmured Miss Ming encouragingly, 'and ...'

Li Pao's voice was almost a shriek: '... only the wounded condemn the pain of others. You see, Ron Ron Ron, I was not—'

'An interesting observation.' Ron Ron Ron put his hands together under his chin. 'Yes, yes, yes. I see.'

'No!' Li Pao took a desperate step forwards, as if to leave.

'By the same argument, Li Pao.' began Ron Ron Ron, and Li Pao became passive, 'you would imply that a strong person who exercised that strength is, in fact, revealing a weakness in his character, eh?'

'No. I ...'

'Oh, but we must have a look at this.' Ron Ron Ron became almost animated. 'It suggests, you see, that indirectly you condemn my efforts as leader of the Symmetrical Fundamentalist Movement in attempting to seize power during the Anarchist Beekeeper period.'

'I assure you, that I was not ...' Li Pao's voice had diminished to a whisper.

'Certainly we were strong enough,' continued Ron Ron Ron. 'If the planet had not, in the meantime, been utilised as a strike-base by some superior alien military force (whose name we never did learn), which killed virtually all opposition and enslaved the remaining third of the human race during the duration of its occupation—not much more than twenty years, admittedly—before they vanished again, either because our part of the galaxy was no longer of strategic importance to them or because their enemies had defeated them, who knows what we could have achieved.'

'Wonders,' gasped Li Pao. 'Wonders, I am sure.'

'You are kind. As it was, Earth was left in a state of semi-barbarism which had no need, I suppose, for the refinements either of Autonomous Hiveism or Symmetrical Fundamentalism, but given the chance I could have—'

'I am sure. I am sure.' Li Pao's voice had taken on the quality of a labouring steam-engine.

'Still,' Ron Ron Ron went on, 'I digress. You see, because of my efforts to parley with the aliens, my motives were misinterpreted—'

'Certainly. Certainly.'

'—and I was forced to use the experimental time craft to flee here. However, my point is this ...'

'Quite, quite, quite ...'

Miss Ming shook her head. 'Oh, you men and your politics. I ...'

But she had not been forceful enough. Ron Ron Ron's (or Ron's Ron's Ron's, as he would have preferred us to write) voice droned on, punctuated by Li Pao's little gasps and sighs. She could not understand Li Pao's allowing himself to be trapped in this awful situation. She had done her best, when he seemed to want to talk to Ron Ron Ron, to begin a conversation that would interest them both, knowing that the only thing the two men had in common was a past taste for political activity and a present tendency, in their impotence, to criticise the shortcomings of their fellows here at the End of Time. But now Li Pao showed no inclination at all to take Ron Ron Ron up on any of his points, which were certainly of no interest to anyone but the Symmetrical Fundamentalist himself. She knew what it was like with some people; if a string was pulled in them, they couldn't stop themselves going on and on. A lot of those she had known, back home in twenty-first century Iowa, it had been like that.

Again, thought Mavis, it was up to her to change the subject. For Li Pao's sake as well as her own.

'... they never did separate properly, you see,' said Ron

Ron Ron.

'Separate?' Miss Ming seized the chance given her by the pause in his monologue. She spoke brightly. 'Properly? Why, that's like my Swiss Cheese Plant. The one I used to have in my office? It grew so big! But the leaves wouldn't separate properly. Is that what happened to yours, Ron Ron Ron?'

'We were discussing strength,' said Ron Ron Ron in some bewilderment.

'Strength! You should have met my ex. I've mentioned him before? Donny Stevens, the heel. Now say what you like about him, but he was *strong*! Betty—you know, that's the friend I told you about?—*more* than a friend really ...' she winked. '... Betty used to say that Donny Stevens was prouder of his pectorals than he was of his prick! Eh?' She shook with laughter.

The two men looked at her in silence.

Li Pao sucked his lower lip.

'And that was saying a lot, where Donny was concerned,' Mavis added.

'Ushshsh ...' said Li Pao.

'Really?' Ron Ron Ron spoke in a peculiar tone.

The silence returned at once. Dutifully, Mavis tried to fill it. She put a hand on Ron Ron Ron's tubular sleeve.

'I shouldn't tell you this, what with my convictions and all—I was polarised in '65, became an all-woman woman, if you get me, after my divorce—but I miss that bastard of a bull sometimes.'

'Well ...' Ron Ron Ron hesitated.

'What this world needs,' said Mavis as she got into her stride, 'if you ask me, is a few more real men. You know? Real men. The girls around here have got more balls than the guys. One real man and, boy!, you'd find my tastes changing just like that ...' She tried, unsuccessfully, to snap her fingers.

'Sssss ...' said Li Pao.

'Anyway,' Mavis was anxious to reassure him that she had not lost track of the original topic, 'it's the same with Swiss Cheese Plants. They're strong. Any conditions will suit them and they'll strangle anything that gets in their way. They use

17

—they *used* to use, I should say—the big ones to fell other trees in Paraquay. I think it's Paraquay. But when it comes to getting the leaves to separate, well, all you can say is that they're bastards to train. Like strong men, I guess. In the end you have to take 'em or leave 'em as they come.'

Mavis laughed again, waiting for their responding laughter, which did not materialise. She was valiant:

'I stayed with my house-plants, but I left that stud to play in his own stable. And how he'd been playing! Betty said if I tried to count the number of mares he'd serviced while *I* thought he was stuck late at the lab I'd need a computer!'

Li Pao and Ron Ron Ron now stood side by side, staring at her.

'*Two* computers!' She had definitely injected a bit of wit into the conversation and given Li Pao a chance to get on to a subject he preferred but evidently neither of them had much of a sense of humour. Li Pao now glanced at his feet. Ron Ron Ron had a silly fixed grin on his face and was just grunting at her, even though she had stopped speaking.

Miss Ming decided to soldier on:

'Did I tell you about the Busy Lizzie that turned out to be Poison Ivy? We were out in the country one day, this was before my divorce—it must have been just after we got married —either '60 or '61—no, it must have been '61 definitely because it was Spring—probably May . . .'

'*Look!*'

Li Pao's voice was so loud that it startled Mavis.

'What?'

'There's Doctor Volospion.' He waved towards where the crowd was thickest. 'He was signalling to you, Miss Ming. Over there!'

The news heartened her. This would be her excuse to get away. But she could, of course, not show Li Pao how pleased she was. So she smiled indulgently. 'Oh, let him wait. Just because he's my host here doesn't mean I have to be at his beck and call the whole time!'

'Please,' said Ron Ron Ron, removing a small, pink, even-fingered hand from a perfectly-square pocket. 'You must not let us, Miss Ming, monopolise your time.'

'Oh, well . . .' She was relieved. 'I'll see you later, perhaps. By-ee.' Her wink was cute; she waggled her fingers at them. But as she turned to seek out Doctor Volospion it seemed that he had disappeared. She turned back and to her surprise saw Li Pao sprinting away from Ron Ron Ron towards the foot of one of Abu Thaleb's monsters, perhaps because he had seen someone to whom he wished to speak. She avoided Ron Ron Ron's eye and set off in the general direction indicated by Li Pao, making her way between guests and wandering elephants who were here in more or less equal numbers.

'At least I did my best,' she said. 'They're very difficult men to talk to.'

She yawned. She was already beginning to be just a trifle bored with the party.

CHAPTER THREE

In which Miss Ming Fails to Find Consolation

The elephants, although the most numerous, were not the largest beasts providing the party's entertainment; its chief feature being the seven monstrous animals who sat on green-brown haunches and raised their heavy heads in mournful song.

These beasts were the pride of Abu Thaleb's collection. They were perfect reproductions of the singing gargantua of Justine IV, a planet long since vanished in the general dissipation of the cosmos (Earth, the reader will remember, had used up a good many other star systems to rejuvenate its own energies).

Abu Thaleb's enthusiasm for elephants and all that was elephantine was so great that he had changed his name to that of the ancient Commissar of Bengal solely because one of that legendary dignitary's other titles had been Lord of All Elephants.

The gargantua were more in the nature of huge baboons, their heads resembling those of Airedale terriers (now, of course, long-extinct) and were so large that the guests standing closest to them could not see them as a whole at all. Moreover, so high were these shaggy heads above the party that the beautiful music of their voices was barely audible.

Elsewhere, the Commissar's guests ate from trays carried upon the backs of baby mammoths, or leaned against the leather hides of hippopotomi which kneeled here and there about the grounds of Abu Thaleb's vast palace, itself fashioned in the shape of two marble elephants standing forehead to forehead, with trunks entwined.

Mavis Ming paused beside a resting oryx and pulled a tiny savoury doughnut or two from its left horn, munching absently as the beast's huge eyes regarded her. 'You look,' she remarked to it, 'as fed up as I feel.' She could find no one to keep her company in that whole cheerful throng. Almost everyone she knew had seemed to turn aside just as she had been about to greet them and Doctor Volospion himself was nowhere to be seen.

'This party,' she continued, 'is definitely tedious.'

'What a supehb fwock, Miss Ming! So fwothy! So yellah!'

Sweet Orb Mace, in flounces and folds of different shades of grey, presented himself before her, smiling and languid. His eyebrows were elaborately arched; his hair incredibly ringletted, his cheeks exquisitely rouged. He made a leg.

The short-skirted yellow dress, with its several petticoats, its baby-blue trimmings (to match her eyes, her best feature), was certainly, Mavis felt, the sexiest thing she had worn for a long while, so she was not surprised by his compliment.

She gave one of her little-girl trills of laughter and pirouetted for him.

'I thought,' she told him, 'that it was high time I felt feminine again. Do you like the bow?' The big blue bow in her honey-blonde hair was trimmed with yellow and matched the smaller bows on her yellow shoes.

'Wondahful!' pronounced Sweet Orb Mace. 'It is quite without compahe!'

She was suddenly much happier. She blew him a kiss and fluttered her lashes. She warmed to Sweet Orb Mace, who could sometimes be such good company (whether as a man or a woman, for his moods varied from day to day) and she took his arm, confiding: 'You know how to flatter a girl. I suppose you, of all people, *should* know. I'll tell you a secret. I've been a bit cunning, you see, in wearing a full skirt. It makes my waist look a little slimmer. I'm the first to admit that I'm not the thinnest girl in the world, but I'm not about to emphasise the fact, am I?'

'Wemahkable.'

Amiably, Sweet Orb Mace strolled in harness while Mavis

whispered further secrets. She told him of the polka-dot elephant she had had when she was seven. She had kept it for years, she said, until it had been run over by a truck, when Donny Stevens had thrown it through the apartment window into the street, during one of their rows.

'I could have taken almost anything else,' she said.

Sweet Orb Mace nodded and murmured little exclamations, but he scarcely seemed to have heard the anecdote. If he had a drawback as a companion, it was his vagueness; his attention wavered so.

'He accused *me* of being childish,' exclaimed Mavis putting, as it were, twice the energy into the conversation, to make up for his failings. 'Ha! He had the mental age of a dirty-minded eleven-year-old! But there you go. I got more love from that elephant than I ever got from Donny Stevens. It's always the people who try to be nice who come in for the nasty treatment, isn't it?'

'Wather!'

'He blamed me for everything. Little Mavis *always* gets the blame! Ever since I was a kid. Everybody's whipping boy, that's Mavis Ming! My father ...'

'Weally?'

She abandoned this line, thinking better of it, and remained with her original sentiment. 'If you don't stand up for yourself, someone'll always step on you. The things I've done for people in the past. And you know what almost always happens?'

'Natuwally ...'

'They turn round and say the cruellest things to you. They always blame you for what they should really be blaming themselves. That woman—Dafnish Armatuce—*well* ...'

'Twagic.'

'Doctor Volospion said I'd been too easy-going with her. I looked after that kid of hers as if it had been my own! It makes you want to give up sometimes, Sweet Orb. But you've got to keep on trying, haven't you? Some of us are fated to suffer ...'

Sweet Orb Mace paused beside a towering mass of ill-smelling hairy flesh which moved rhythmically and shook the surrounding ground so that little fissures appeared. It was the gently tapping toe of one of Abu Thaleb's singing gargantua. Sweet Orb Mace stared gravely up, unable to see the head of the beast. 'Oh, cehtainly,' he agreed. 'Pwetty tune, don't you think?'

She lifted an ear, but shrugged. 'No, I don't.'

He was mildly surprised.

'Too much like a dirge for my taste,' she said. 'I like something catchy.' She sighed, her mood returning to its former state. 'Oh, dear! This is a very boring party.'

He became astonished.

'This pwofusion of pachyderms bohwing? Oh, no! I find it fascinating, Miss Ming. An extwavagance of elephants, a genewosity of giants!'

She could not agree. Her eye, perhaps, was jaundiced.

Sweet Orb Mace, sensing her displeasure, became anxious. 'Still,' he added, 'evewyone knows how easily impwessed I am. Such a poah imagination of my own, you know.'

She sighed. 'I expected more.'

'Monsters?' He glanced about, as if to find her some. 'Awgonheart Po has yet to make his contwibution! He is wumouhed to be supplying the main feast.'

'I didn't know.' She sighed again. 'It's not that. I was hoping to meet some nice person. Someone—you know—I could have a real relationship with. I guess I expected too much from that Dafnish and her kid—but it's, well, turnéd me onto the *idea*. I'm unfulfilled as a woman, Sweet Orb Mace, if you want the raw truth of it.'

She looked expectantly at her elegantly poised escort.

'Tut,' said Sweet Orb Mace abstractedly. 'Tut, tut.' He still stared skywards.

She raised her voice. 'You're not, I guess, in the mood yourself. I'm going to go home if things don't perk up. If you feel like coming back now—or dropping round later ...? I'm still staying at Doctor Volospion's.'

'Weally?'

She laughed at herself. 'I should try to sound more positive,

23

shouldn't I? Nobody's going to respond well to a faltering approach like that. Well, Sweet Orb Mace, what about it?'

'It?'

She was actually depressed now.

'I meant ...'

'I pwomised to meet O'Kala Incarnadine heah,' said Sweet Orb Mace. 'I was suah—ah—and theah he is!' carolled her companion. 'If you will excuse me, Miss Ming ...' Another elaborate bending of the body, a sweep of the hand.

'Oh, sure,' she murmured.

Sweet Orb Mace rose a few feet into the air and drifted towards O'Kala Incarnadine, who had come as a rhinoceros.

'The way I'm beginning to feel,' said Miss Ming to herself, 'even O'Kala Incarnadine's looking attractive. Bye, bye, Sweet Orb. No sweat. Oh, Christ! This boredom is *killing*!'

And then she had seen her protector, her host, her mentor, her Guardian Angel and, with a grateful 'Hi!', she flew.

Doctor Volospion was sighted at last! He seemed at times like this her only stability. He it was who had first found her when, in her time machine, dazed and frightened, she had arrived at the End of Time. Doctor Volospion had claimed her for his menagerie, thinking from her conversation that she belonged to some religious order (she had been delirious) and had discovered only later that she was a simple historian who believed that she had returned to the past, to the Middle Ages. He had been disappointed but had treated her courteously and now allowed her the full run of his house. She did not fit into his menagerie which was religious in emphasis, consisting of nuns, prophets, gods, demons and so forth. She could have founded her own establishment, had she wished, but she preferred the security of his sometimes dolorous domicile.

She slowed her pace. Doctor Volospion was hailing the Commissar of Bengal, whose howdah-shaped golden air cab was drifting back to the ground (apparently, Abu Thaleb had been feeding his gigantic pets).

'Coo-ee!' cried Miss Ming as she approached.

But Doctor Volospion had not heard her.

'Coo-ee.'

He joined in conversation with Abu Thaleb.

'Coo-ee, Doctor!'

Now the sardonic, saturnine features turned to regard her. The sleek black head moved in a kind of bow and the corners of the thin, red mouth lifted.

She was panting as she reached them. 'It's only little me!'

Abu Thaleb was avuncular. 'Miss Ming, again we meet. Scheherazade come among us.' The dusky Commissar was one of the few regular visitors to Doctor Volospion's, perhaps the only friend of the Doctor's to treat her kindly. 'You enjoy the entertainment, I hope?'

'It's a great party if you like elephants,' she said. But the joke had misfired; Abu Thaleb was frowning. So she added with some eagerness: 'I personally *love* elephants.'

'I did not know we had that in common.'

'Oh, yes. When I was a little girl I used to go for rides at the zoo whenever I could. At least once a year, on my birthday. My daddy would try to take me, no matter what else was happening ...'

'I must join in the compliments.' Doctor Volospion cast a glinting eye from her toes to her bow. 'You outshine us all, Miss Ming. Such taste! Such elegance! We, in our poor garb, are mere flickering candles to your super-nova!'

Her giggle of response was hesitant, as if she suspected him of satire, but then an expression almost of tranquillity passed across her features. His flattery appeared to have a euphoric effect upon her. She became a fondled cat.

'Oh, you always do it to me, Doctor Volospion. Here I am trying to be brittle and witty, cool and dignified, and you make me grin and blush like a schoolgirl.'

'Forgive me.'

She frowned, finger to lips. 'I'm trying to think of a witticism to please you.'

'Your presence is uniquely pleasing, Miss Ming.'

Doctor Volospion moved his thin arms which were hardly able to bear the weight of the sleeves of his black and gold brocade gown.

'But ...'

25

Doctor Volospion turned to Abu Thaleb. 'You bring us a world of gentle monsters, exquisite Commissar. Gross of frame, mild of manner, delicate of spirit, your paradoxical pachyderms!'

'They are very *practical* beasts, Doctor Volospion.' Abu Thaleb spoke defensively, as if he, too, suspected irony.

People would often respond in this way to Doctor Volospion's remarks which were almost always, on the surface at least, bland enough.

'Oh, indeed!' Doctor Volospion eyed a passing calf which had paused and was tentatively extending its trunk to accept a piece of fruit from the Commissar's open palm. 'Servants of Man since the Beginning of Time.'

'Worshipped as Gods in many eras and climes ...' added Abu Thaleb.

'Gods! True. Ganesh ...'

Abu Thaleb had lost his reservations:

'I have recreated examples of every known species! The English, the Bulgarian, the Chinese, and, of course the Indian ...'

'You have a favourite?' Volospion heaved at a sleeve and scratched an eyebrow.

'My favourites are the Swiss Alpine elephants. There is one now. Notice its oddly shaped hooves. These were the famous White Elephants of Sitting Bull, used in the Liberation of Chicago in the fiftieth century.'

Miss Ming felt bound to interrupt. 'Are you absolutely certain of that, Commissar? The story sounds a bit familiar, but isn't quite right. I am an historian, after all, if not a very good one. You're not thinking of Carthage ... ?' She became confused, apparently afraid that she had offended him again. 'I'm sorry. I shouldn't have butted in. You know what a silly little ignoramus I am ...'

'I am absolutely certain, my dear,' said Abu Thaleb kindly. 'I had most of the information from an old tape which Jherek Carnelian found for me in one of the rotting cities. The translation might not have been perfect, but ...'

'Ah, so Carthage could have sounded like Chicago, particularly after it has been through a number of transcriptions. You see *Sitting* Bull could have been—'

Doctor Volospion broke in on her speculations. 'What romantic times those must have been! Your own stories, Miss Ming, are redolent with the atmosphere of our glorious and vanished past!' He 'looked at Abu Thaleb as he spoke. Abu Thaleb moved uncomfortably.

Mavis Ming laughed. 'Well, it wasn't all fun, you know.' She sighed with pleasure, addressing Abu Thaleb. 'The thing I like about Doctor Volospion is the way he always lets me talk. He's always *interested* . . .'

Abu Thaleb avoided both their eyes.

'Say what you like about him,' she continued, 'Doctor Volospion's a gentleman!' She became serious. 'No, in a lot of ways the past was hell, though I must say there were satisfactions I never realised I'd miss till now. Sex, for instance.'

'You mean sexual pleasure?' The Commissar of Bengal drew a banana from his quilted cuff and began to peel it.

Miss Ming appeared to be taken aback by this gesture. Her voice was distant. 'I certainly do mean that.'

'Oh, surely . . .' murmured Doctor Volospion.

Miss Ming found her old voice. 'Nobody around here ever seems to be interested. I mean really interested. If that's what's meant by an ancient race, give me what you call the Dawn Ages—my time—any day of the week! Well, not that you have days or weeks, but you know what I mean. Real sex!'

She seemed to realise that she was in danger of becoming intense and she tried to lighten the effect of her speech by breaking into what, in the Dawn Age, might have been a musical laugh.

When her laughter had died away, Doctor Volospion touched his right index finger to his left eyelid. 'Can this be true, Miss Ming?'

'Oh, you're a sweetie, Doctor Volospion. You make a girl feel really foolish sometimes. It's not your fault. You've got what we used to call an "unfortunate tone"—it seems to make a mockery of everything. I know what it is. You don't have to tell me. You're really quite shy, like me. I've lived with you long enough to know ...'

'I am honoured, as always, by your interpretation of my character. But I am genuinely curious. I can think of so many who concern themselves with little else but sexual gratification. My Lady Charlotina, O'Kala Incarnadine, Gaf the Horse in Tears and, of course, Mistress Christia, the Everlasting Concubine.' He cast an eye over the surrounding guests. 'Jherek Carnelian *crucifies* himself in pursuit of his sexual object ...'

'It's not what I meant,' she explained. 'You see they only *play* at it. They're not really *motivated* by it. It's hard to explain.' She became coy. 'Anyway, I don't think any of those are my types, actually.'

The Commissar of Bengal finished feeding his banana to a passing pachyderm. 'I seem to recall that you were quite struck by My Lady Charlotina at one time, Miss Ming,' he said.

'Oh, that was—'

Doctor Volospion studied something beyond her left shoulder. 'And then there was that other lady. The time traveller, who I rather took to, myself. Why, we were almost rivals for a while. *You* were in love, you said, Miss Ming.'

'Oh, now you're being cruel! I'd rather you didn't mention ...'

'Of course.' Now he looked beyond her right shoulder. 'A tragedy.'

'It's not that I—I mean, I don't like to think. I was badly let down by Dafnish—and by Snuffles, in particular. How was I to know that ... Well, if you hadn't consoled me then, I don't know what I'd have done. But I wish you wouldn't bring it up. Not here, at least. Oh, people can be so *baffling* sometimes. I'm not perfect, I know, but I do my best to be tactful. To look on the bright side. To help others. Betty used to say that I ought to think more of my *own* interests. She said I wasn't selfish enough. Oh, dear—people must think me a terrible fool. When they think of me at *all*!' She sniffed. 'I'm sorry ...'

She craned to look back, following Doctor Volospion's gaze.

Li Pao was nearby, bowing briefly to Doctor Volospion,

making as if to pass on, for he was apparently in some haste, but Doctor Volospion smilingly called him over.

'I was complimenting our host on his collection,' he explained to Li Pao.

Abu Thaleb made a modest gesture.

Miss Ming bit her lip.

Li Pao cleared his throat.

'Aren't they fine?' said Doctor Volospion.

'It is pleasant to see the beasts working,' Li Pao said pointedly, 'if only for the delight of these drones.'

Doctor Volospion's smile broadened. 'Ah, Li Pao, as usual you refuse amusement! Still, that's your recreation I suppose, or you would not attend so many of our parties.'

Li Pao bridled. 'I come, Doctor Volospion, on principle. Occasionally, there is one who will listen to me for a few moments. My conscience drives me here. One day perhaps I will begin to convince you of the value of moral struggle.'

An affectionate trunk nuzzled his oriental ear. He moved his head.

Doctor Volospion was placatory. 'I *am* convinced, Li Pao, my dear friend. Its value to the twenty-seventh century is immeasurable. But here we are at the End of Time and we have quite different needs. Our future is uncertain, to say the least. The cosmos contracts and perishes and soon we must perish with it. Will industry put a stop to the dissolution of the Universe? I think not.'

Miss Ming patted at a blonde curl.

'Then you fear the end?' Li Pao said with some satisfaction.

Doctor Volospion affected a yawn. 'Fear? What is that?'

Li Pao's chuckle was grim. 'Oh, it's rare enough here, but I think you reveal at least a touch of it, Doctor Volospion.'

'Fear!' Doctor Volospion's nostrils developed a contemptuous flare. 'You suggest that I—? But this is such a baseless observation. An accusation, even!'

'I do not accuse, Doctor Volospion. I do not denigrate. Fear, where real danger threatens, is surely a sane enough response? A healthy one? Is it insane to ignore the knife which strikes for the heart?'

29

'Knife? Heart?' Abu Thaleb lured the persistent elephant towards him, holding a bunch of grapes. 'Do forgive me, Li Pao ...'

Doctor Volospion said softly: 'I think, Li Pao, that you will have to consider me insane.'

Li Pao would not relent. 'No! You are afraid. Your denials display it, your posture pronounces it!'

Doctor Volospion moved an overloaded shoulder. 'Such instincts, you see, have atrophied at the End of Time. You credit your own feelings to me, I think.'

Li Pao's gaze was steady. 'I am not deceived, Doctor Volospion. What are you? Time traveller or space traveller? You are no more born of this Age than am I, or Miss Ming, here.'

'What—?' Doctor Volospion was alerted.

'You say that you do not fear,' continued the Chinese. 'Yet you hate well enough, that's plain. Your hatred of Lord Jagged, for instance, is patent. And you exhibit jealousies and vanities that are unknown, say, to the Duke of Queens. If these are innocent of true guile, you are not. It is why I know there is a point in my talking to you.'

'I will not be condescended to!' Doctor Volospion glared.

'I repeat—I praise these emotions. In their place—'

'Praise?' Doctor Volospion raised both his hands, palms outward, to bring a pause. His voice, almost a whisper, threatened. 'Strange flattery, indeed! You go too far, Li Pao. The manners of your own time would never allow such insults.'

'I do think you've gone just a teeny bit too far, Li Pao.' Mavis Ming was anxious to reduce the tension. 'Why are you so bent on baiting Doctor Volospion. He's done nothing to you.'

'You refuse to admit it,' Li Pao continued relentlessly, 'but we face the death of everything. Thus I justify my directness.'

'Shall we die gracelessly, then? Pining for hope when there is none? Whining for salvation when we are beyond help? You are offensive at every level, Li Pao.'

Miss Ming was desperate to destroy this atmosphere. 'Oh, look over there!' she cried. 'Can it be Argonheart Po arrived at last, with the food?'

'He *is* late,' said Abu Thaleb, looking up from his elephant.

Li Pao and Doctor Volospion both ignored this sidetracking.

'There *is* hope, if we work,' said Li Pao.

'What? This is unbelievable.' Doctor Volospion sought an ally but found only the anxious eyes of Mavis Ming. He avoided them. 'The end looms—the inevitable beckons. Death comes stalking over the horizon. Mortality returns to the Earth after an absence of millenia. And you speak of what? Of work? Work!' Doctor Volospion's laugh was harsh. 'Work? For what? This age is called the End of Time for good reason, Li Pao! We have run our race. Soon we shall all be ash on the cosmic wind.'

'But if a few of us were to consider . . .'

'Forgive me, Li Pao, but you bore me. I have had my fill of bores today.'

'You boys should really stop squabbling like this.' Determinedly, Mavis Ming adopted a matronly role. 'Silly, gloomy talk. You're making me feel quite depressed. What possible good can it do for anyone? Let's have a bit more cheerfulness, eh? Did I ever tell you about the time I—well, I was about fourteen, and I'd done it for a dare—we got caught in the church by the Reverend Kovac—I'd told Sandy, that was my friend—'

Doctor Volospion's temper was not improved. An expression of pure horror bloomed on her round face as she realised that she had made another misjudgement and caused her protector to turn on her.

He was vicious. 'The role of diplomat, Miss Ming, does not greatly suit you.'

'Oh!'

Abu Thaleb became aware, at last, of the ambience. 'Come now . . .'

'You will be kind enough not to interfere, not to interject your absurd and pointless anecdotes into the conversation, Miss Ming!'

'*Doctor Volospion!*' It was a shriek of betrayal. Miss Ming took a step backwards. She became afraid.

'Oh, she meant no harm ...' Li Pao was in no position to mediate.

'How,' inquired Doctor Volospion of the shaking creature, 'would you suggest we settle our dispute, Miss Ming? With swords, like Lord Shark and the Duke of Queens? With pistols? Reverb-guns? Flame-lances?'

Her throat quivered. 'I didn't mean ...'

'Well? Hm?' His long chin pointed at her throat. 'Speak up, my portly referee. Tell us!'

She had become very pale and yet her cheeks flamed with humiliation and she did not dare look at any of them. 'I was only trying to help. You were so angry, both of you, and there's no need to lose your tempers ...'

'Angry? You are witless, madam. Could you not see that we jested?'

There was no evidence. Miss Ming became confused.

Li Pao's lips were pursed, his cheeks were as pale as hers were red. Doctor Volospion's eyes were hard and fiery. Abu Thaleb gave vent to a troubled muttering.

Miss Ming seemed fixed in her position by a terrible fascination. Mindlessly, she stared at the eyes of her accuser. It seemed that her urge to flee was balanced by her compulsion to stay, to fan these flames, to produce the holocaust that would consume her, and her mouth opened and words fled out of it, high and frightened:

'Not a very funny joke, I must say, calling someone fat and stupid. Make up your mind, Doctor Volospion. Only a minute or two ago you said how nice I looked. Don't pick on little Mavis, just because you're losing your argument!' She panted. 'Oh!'

She cast about for friends, but all eyes were averted, save Volospion's, and those pierced.

'Oh!' she said again.

Doctor Volospion parted his teeth a fraction, to hiss:

'I should be more than grateful, Miss Ming, if you would be silent. For once in your life I suggest that you reflect on your own singular lack of sensitivity—'

32

'Oh!'

'—on your inability to interpret the slightest nuance of social intercourse save in your own unsavoury terms.'

'O-oh!'

'A psychic cripple, Miss Ming, has no business swimming in the fast-running rivers of philosophical discussion.'

'Volospion!' Li Pao made a hesitant movement.

Perhaps Miss Ming did not hear his words at all, perhaps she only experienced his tone, his vicious stance. 'You *are* in a bad mood today . . .' she began, and then words gave way to her strangled, half-checked sobs.

'Volospion! Volospion! You round on that wretch because you cannot answer me!'

'Ha!' Doctor Volospion turned slowly, hampered by his robes.

Abu Thaleb had been observing Miss Ming. He spoke conversationally, leaning forward to stare at her face, his huge, feathered turban nodding. 'Are those tears, my dear?'

She snorted.

'I had heard of elephants weeping,' said Abu Thaleb with some animation. 'Or was it giraffes?—but I never thought to have the chance to witness . . .'

His tone produced a partial recovery in her. She lifted a wounded face. 'Oh, be quiet! You and your stupid elephants.'

'So, all our time travellers are blessed with the same brand of good manners, it seems.' Volospion had become cool. 'I fear we have yet to grasp the essence of your social customs, madam.'

She trembled.

'Childish irony . . .' said Li Pao.

'Oh, stop it, Li Pao!' Mavis flinched away from him. 'You started all this.'

'Well, perhaps . . .'

Abu Thaleb put a puzzled tongue to his lower lip. 'If . . .'

'Oh,' she sobbed, 'I'm so *sorry*, Commissar. I'm sorry, Doctor Volospion. I didn't mean to . . .'

'It is we who are in the wrong,' Li Pao told her. 'I should have known better. You are a troubled young girl at heart . . .'

Her weeping grew mightier.

Doctor Volospion, Abu Thaleb and Li Pao now stood around her, looking down at her.

'Come, come,' said Abu Thaleb. He patted the crown of her head.

'Oh, I'm sorry. I was only trying to help ... Why does it always have to be me ...?'

Doctor Volospion at last placed a hand on her arm. 'Perhaps I had best escort you home?' He was magnanimous. 'You should rest.'

'Oh!' She moved to him, as if to be comforted, and then withdrew. 'Oh, you're right! You're right! I'm fat. I'm stupid. I'm ugly.' She pulled away from him.

'No, no ...' murmured Abu Thaleb. 'I think that you are immensely attractive ...'

She raised a trembling chin. 'It's all right.' She swallowed. 'I'm fine now.'

Abu Thaleb gave a sigh of relief. The other two, however, continued to watch her.

She sniffed. 'I just didn't want to see anyone having a bad time, hurting one another. Yes, you're right, Doctor Volospion. I shouldn't have come. I'll go home.'

Doctor Volospion replaced his hand, to steady her. His voice was low and calming. 'Good. I will take you in my air car.'

'No. You stay and enjoy yourself. It's my fault. I'm very sorry.'

'You are too distraught.'

'Perhaps I should take her,' said Li Pao. 'After all, I introduced the original argument.'

'We all relieve the boredom in one way or another,' said Doctor Volospion quietly. 'I should not have responded as I did.'

'Nonsense. You had every reason ...'

'Boo-hoo,' said Miss Ming. She had broken down again.

Abu Thaleb said coaxingly: 'Would you like one of my little flying elephants, my dear, for your very own? You could take it with you.'

'Oh-ah-ha-ha . . .'

'Poor thing,' said Abu Thaleb. 'I think she would have been better off in a menagerie, Doctor Volospion. Some of them feel much safer there, you know. Our world is too difficult for them to grasp. Now, if I were you . . .'

Doctor Volospion tightened his grip.

'Oh!'

'You are too sensitive, Miss Ming,' said Li Pao. 'You must not take us seriously.'

Doctor Volospion laughed. 'Is that so, Li Pao?'

'I meant . . .'

'Ah, look!' Doctor Volospion raised a hand to point. 'Here's your friend, Miss Ming.'

'Friend?' Red eyes were raised. Another sniff.

'Your friend, the cook.'

It was Argonheart Po, in smock and cap of dark brown and scarlet, so corpulent as to make Miss Ming look slim. He advanced towards them with monumental dignity, pushing small elephants from his path. With a brief bow he acknowledged the company and then addressed Abu Thaleb.

'I have come to apologise, epicurian Commissar, for the lateness of my contribution.'

'No, no . . .' Abu Thaleb seemed weary of what appeared to be a welter of regrets.

'There is an integral fault in my recipe,' explained the Master Chef, 'which I am loathe to disguise by any artifice . . .'

The Commissar of Bengal waved a white-gloved hand. 'You are too modest, Kaiser of Kitchens. You are too much a perfectionist. I am certain that none of us would detect any discrepancy . . .'

Argonheart Po acknowledged the compliment with a smile. 'Possibly. But *I* would know.' He confided to the others: 'The cry of the artist, I fear, down the Ages. I hope, Abu Thaleb, that things will right themselves before long. If not, I shall bring you those confections which have been successful, but I will abandon the rest.'

'Drastic . . .' Abu Thaleb lowered his eyes and shook his head. 'Can we not help in some way?'

'The very reason I came. I hoped to gain an opinion. If there is someone who could find it within themselves to leave the party for a short while, to return with me and sample my creations, not so much for their flavour as for their consistency. It would not require much time, nor would it require a particularly sophisticated palate, but ...'

'Miss Ming!' said Doctor Volospion.

'Me,' she said.

'Here is your chance to be of service.'

'Well,' she began, 'as everyone knows, I'm no gourmet. Not that I don't enjoy my chow, and, of course, Argonheart's is always excellent, but I'd like to help out, if I can.' She was twice the woman.

'It is not a gourmet's opinion I seek,' Argonheart Po told her. 'You will do excellently, Miss Ming, if you can spare a little time.'

'You would be delighted, wouldn't you, Miss Ming?' said Abu Thaleb sympathetically.

'Delighted,' she confirmed. She cast a wary glance at Doctor Volospion. 'You wouldn't mind?'

'Certainly not!' He was almost effusive.

'A splendid idea,' said Li Pao, blatantly relieved.

'Well, then, I shall be your taster, Argonheart.' She linked her arm in the cook's. 'And I really am sorry for that silly fuss, everybody.'

They shook their heads. They waved their fingers.

She smiled. 'It did clear the air, anyway, didn't it? You're all friends again now.'

'Absolutely,' said Li Pao.

'Well, that's fine.'

'And you won't be wanting the little elephant?' Abu Thaleb asked. 'I can always create another.'

'I'd *love* one, Abu. Another time, perhaps when I have a menagerie of my own. And power rings of my own and everything. I've nowhere to keep it while I stay with Doctor Volospion.'

'Ah, well.' Abu Thaleb also seemed relieved.

'I think,' said Argonheart Po, 'that we should go as quickly as possible.'

'Of course,' she said, 'you really must take me in hand, Argonheart, and tell me exactly what you expect me to do.'

'An opinion, I assure you, is all I seek.'

They made their adieux.

'*Well*,' she confided to Argonheart as they left, 'I must say you turned up at just the right moment. Honestly, I've never *seen* such a display of temper! You're so calm, Argonheart. So unshakeably dignified, you know? I did my best, of course, to calm everyone down, but they were just *determined* to have a row! Of course, I do blame Li Pao. Doctor Volospion had a perfectly understandable point of view, but would Li Pao listen to him? Not a bit of it. I suspect that Li Pao never listens to anyone but himself. He can be so thoughtless sometimes, don't you find that?'

The Master Chef smacked his lips.

CHAPTER FOUR

*In which Mavis Ming is once again Disappointed
in her Ambitions*

Argonheart Po dipped his fingers into his rainbow plesiosaurus
(sixty distinct flavours of gelatine) and withdrew it as the
beast turned its long neck round to investigate, mildly, the
source of the irritation.

The great cook put hand to mouth, sucked, and sighed.

'What a shame! Such an excellent taste.'

His creature, lumbering on massive legs that were still somewhat wobbly, having failed to set at the same time as the rest
of its bulk, moved to rejoin the herd grazing some distance
away on the especially prepared trees of pastry and angelica
Argonheart Po had designed to occupy them until it was time
to drive them to the party which was only a mile or two off
(the gargantua were plainly visible on the horizon).

'You agree, then, Miss Ming? The legs lack coherence.' He
licked a disappointed mouth.

'Isn't there something you could add?' she suggested.
'Those flippers were really meant for the sea, you know ...'

'Mm?'

'It's not your fault, not strictly speaking. The design of the
creature itself is wrong. You must be able to do *something*,
Argonheart, dear.'

'Oh, indeed. A twist of a power ring and all would be well,
but I should continue to be haunted by the mystery. Was the
temperature too high, for instance? You see, I allow for all the
possibilities. My researches show that the animal could move
on land. I wonder if the weight of the beast alters the atomic
structure of the gelatine. If so, I should have prepared for it,

in my original recipe. There is no time to begin again.'

'But Argonheart . . .'

He shook his huge head. 'I must cull the herd of the failures and present, I am afraid, only a partial spectacle.'

'Abu Thaleb will still be pleased, I'm sure.'

'I hope so.' He voiced a stupendous and sultry sigh.

'It *is* nice to be out of the hurly burly for a bit,' she told him, her mind moving on to other topics.

'If you would care to rejoin the party now?'

'No. I want to be here with you. That is, if you have no objection to little Mavis watching a real artist at work.'

'Of course.'

She smiled at him. 'It's such a relief, you see, to be out here alone with a real man. With someone who *does* something.'

She simpered. 'What I mean is, Argonheart, is that I've always wanted . . .'

She gasped as he jumped, his hands flailing, to taste a passing pterodactyl. He missed it by several inches, staggered and fell to one knee.

'Cunning beasts, those.' He picked himself up. 'My fault. I should have made them easier to catch. Too much sherry and not enough blancmange.'

She sidled up to him again. 'My husband, Donny Stevens, was a real man, for all his faults.'

Argonheart returned suddenly to his knees. He cupped his hands around something which wobbled, glinting green and yellow in the pale sunshine. 'Oh, this makes up for everything. See what it is, Miss Ming?'

'A dollop of jello?'

'Dollop? *Dollop!*' He breathed upon it. He fondled the rounded, quivering surface. He spoke reverently. 'This is an egg, Miss Ming. One of my creations has actually laid an egg. Good heavens! I could breed them. What an achievement!' His expression became seraphic.

'A man like you is capable of anything, Argonheart. I often felt Donny was like that. I never thought I'd miss the bastard.'

He was searching the ground for more eggs.

'You remind me of him a little,' she said softly. 'You are

real, Argonheart.'

Argonheart Po's only weakness was for metaphysical speculation. Miss Ming had captured his attention. Stroking his
egg, he looked round. 'Mm?'

Her breast rose and fell rapidly. 'A real man.'

He was curious. 'You believe everyone else imaginary,
then? But why should I be real when the others are not? Why
should *you* be real? Reality, after all, can be the syllabub
that melts upon the tongue, leaving not even a flavour of
memory ...'

Her breathing became calmer. She turned to contemplate
the half-melted remains of a completely unsuccessful stego-
saurus.

'I meant,' she said, 'that Danny was a manly man. Stupid
and vain, of course. But that's all part of it. And obsessed with
his work—well, when he wasn't screwing his assistants.' She
laid her hand upon his trembling egg. 'I like you, Argonheart.
Have you ever thought ... ?'

But the chef's attention was wavering again as he bent to
scoop up a little iguanadon. He placed his egg carefully upon a
slab of marzipan rock and held the iguanadon out to her for
her inspection.

With a frustrated sigh she licked the beast's slippery neck.
'Too much lime for my taste.'

She gave a theatrical shudder and laughed. 'Far too bitter
for me, Argonheart, dear.'

'But the texture? It was the texture, alone, I needed to
know about.'

The iguanadon struggled, squawking rather like a chicken,
and was released. It ran, glistening, semi-transparent, green
and orange, in a crazy path towards the near-by cola lake.

'Perfect,' she said. 'Firm and juicy.'

He nodded sadly. 'The small ones are by far the most successful. But that will scarcely satisfy Abu Thaleb. I meant the
monsters for him. The little beasts were only to set off the
large ones—to set the scale, do you see. I was too ambitious,
Miss Ming. I tried to produce too much and too many.' His
fat brow wrinkled.

'You haven't been listening, Argonheart, dear,' she chided. 'Argonheart?'

Reluctantly he withdrew from his regrets. 'We were discussing the nature of reality.'

'No.'

'You were discussing what? Men?'

She patted at the yellow flounces of her frock. 'Or their absence?' She chuckled. 'I could do with one ...'

He had picked up a ladle in his plump, gloved hand. She followed him as he approached his lake, bent on a final taste.

'A man? What could you do with one?' He sipped.

'I need one.'

'A special kind?'

'A real one.'

'Couldn't you make something—someone, I mean—to suit you? Doctor Volospion would help.' He looked across the tranquil surface, like molten amber. 'Delicious!'

She seemed pained. 'There's no need, dear, to throw that particular episode in my face.'

'Um. Yet, I'm indulging myself, I fear.' He stooped, dipped his ladle, drew it to his red lips, sampled self-critically and nodded his head. 'Yes. The conception was too grandiose. Given another day I could put everything to rights, but poor Abu Thaleb expects ... Ah, well!'

'Forget all about that for a moment.' Lust was mounting in her. She slipped a hand along his massive thigh. 'Make love to me, Argonheart. I've been so unhappy.'

He rubbed his several chins. 'Oh, I see.'

'You knew all along, didn't you? What I wanted?'

'Um.'

'You're so proud, Argonheart. So masculine. A lot of girls don't like fat men, but I do.' She giggled. 'It's what they used to say about me. All the more to get hold of. Please, Argonheart, please!'

'My confections,' he murmured lamely.

'You can spare a few minutes, surely?' She dug her nails into his chest. 'Argonheart!'

'They could—'

'You must relax sometime. You have to relax. It gives you a new perspective.'

'Well, yes, that's true.'

'Argonheart!' She moved against him.

'I certainly cannot improve anything now. Perhaps you are right. Yes ...'

'Yes! You'll feel so much better. And I will, too.'

'Possibly ...'

'Definitely!'

She pulled him towards a pile of discarded dark brown straw. 'Here's a good place.' She sank into it, tugging at his gloved hand.

'What?' he murmured. 'In the vermicelli?'

It was already begining to stick to her sweating arms, but it was plain that such considerations were no longer important. 'Why not? Why not? Oh, my darling. Oh, Argonheart!'

He drew off his gloves. He reached down and removed a strand or two of the vermicelli from her elbow and placed it neatly on her neck. He stood back.

She writhed in the chocolate.

'Argonheart!' She mewed.

With a shrug, he fell beside her in the chocolate.

It was at the point where she had helped him to drag the tight scarlet smock up to his navel while wriggling her own blue lace knickers to just below her knees that they heard a shriek that filled the sky and saw the crimson spaceship falling through the dark blue heavens in an aura of multi-coloured flame.

Argonheart's belly quivered against her as he paused.

'Golly!' said Mavis Ming.

Argonheart licked her shoulder, but his attention was no longer with her. He glanced back. The spaceship was still falling. The noise was immense.

'Don't stop,' she said. 'There's still time. It won't take long.'

But Argonheart was already rolling over in the vermicelli, pulling his smock back into position. He stood up. Shreds of half-melted confectionery dropped from his legs.

A dreadful wail escaped Miss Ming. It was drowned by the

42

roar of the ship.

With her fist she pounded at the vermicelli. It flew in all directions. She appeared to be swearing. And then, when the ship's noise had dropped momentarily to a muted howl, and as Mavis Ming drew up her underwear, her voice, disappointed, despairing, could be heard again.

'What a moment to pick! Poor old Mavis. Isn't it just your luck.'

CHAPTER FIVE

*In which Certain Denizens at the End of Time
Indulge Themselves in Speculation
as to the Nature of the Visitor from
Space*

It was a spaceship from some mythical antiquity, all fins and
flutes and glittering bubbles, tapering at the nose, bulbous at
the base, where its rockets roared. It slowed as they watched,
falling with a peculiar swaying motion, as if its engines mal-
functioned, the vents first on one side and then on the other
sputtering, gouting, sputtering again until, just before the ship
reached the ground, the rockets flared in unison, bouncing the
machine like a ball on a water jet, gradually subsiding until it
had settled to earth.

Miss Ming, observing it from her nest of chocolate worms,
tightened her lips.

Even after the ship had landed, flame still rolled around its
hull, sensuous flame caressing the scarlet metal.

The surrounding terrain sent up heavy black smoke, crackling as if to protest. The smoke curled close to the ground,
moving towards the ship: eels attracted to wreckage.

Miss Ming was in no temper to admire the machine; she
glared at it.

'It has a certain authority, the ship,' murmured Argonheart
Po.

'A fine sense of timing, I must say! A little lovemaking
would have improved my spirits no end and taken away the
nasty taste of Doctor Volospion's tantrum. It isn't as if I get
the chance every day and I haven't had a man for ages. I don't
even know if one can still give me what I need! Even you,

44

Argonheart . . .'

She pouted, brushing at the nasty sticky stuff clinging to her petticoats. 'I'm too furious to speak!'

Argonheart Po helped her from the pile and, perhaps moved by unconscious chivalry, pecked her upon the cheek. The smell of burning filled the air.

'Ugh,' she said. 'What a *stink*, too!'

'It is the least attractive of odours,' Argonheart said.

'It's horrible. Surely it can't just be coming from that ship?'

The heat from the vessel was heavy on their skins. Argonheart Po, had his body been so fashioned, would have been sweating quite as much as Miss Ming. His sensitive nose twitched.

'There is something familiar about it,' he agreed, 'which I would not normally identify with hot metal.' He perused the landscape. His cry of horror echoed over it.

'Ah! Look what it has done! Look! Oh, it is too bad!'

Miss Ming looked and saw nothing. 'What?'

Argonheart was in anguish. His hands clenched, his eyes blazed.

'It has melted half my dinosaurs. That is what is making the smoke!'

Argonheart Po began to roll rapidly in the direction of the ship, Mavis Ming forgotten.

'Hey!' she cried. 'What if there's danger?'

He had not heard her.

With a whimper, she followed him.

'Murderer!' cried the distressed chef. 'Philistine!' He shook his fist at the ship. He danced about it, forced back by its heat. He attempted to kick it and failed.

'Locust!' he raved. 'Ravager! Insensitive despoiler!'

His energy dissipated, he fell to his knees in the glutinous mess. He wept. 'Oh, my monsters! My jellies!'

Mavis Ming hovered a short distance away. She wore the pout of someone who considered themselves abandoned in their hour of need.

'Argonheart!' she called.

'Burned! All burned!'

'Argonheart, we don't know what sort of creatures are *in* that spaceship. They could mean us harm!'

'Ruin, ruin, ruin ...'

'Argonheart. I think we should go and warn someone, don't you?' She discovered that her lovely shoes were stuck. As she lifted her feet, long strands of toffee-like stuff came with them. She waded back to a patch of dust still free of melted dinosaur.

Her attention focused upon the ship as curiosity conquered caution. 'I've seen alien spacecraft before,' she said. 'Lots of them. But this doesn't look alien at all. It's got a distinctly human look to it, in fact.'

Argonheart Po raised his mighty body to its feet and, with shoulders bowed, mourned his dead creations.

'Argonheart, don't you think it's got a rather *romantic* appearance, really?'

Argonheart Po turned his back on the source of his anger and folded his arms across his chest. He wore a martyred air, yet his dignity increased.

Mavis Ming continued to inspect the spaceship. A strange smile had replaced the expression of anxiety she had worn earlier. 'Come to think of it, it's just the sort of ship I used to read about when I was a little girl. All the space-heroes had ships like that.' She became fey. 'Perhaps at long last my prayers have been answered, Argonheart.'

The Master Chef grunted. He was lost in profundity.

Miss Ming uttered her trilling laugh. 'Has my handsome space-knight arrived to carry me off, do you think? To the wonderful planet of Paradise V?'

From Argonheart there issued a deep, violent rumbling, as of an angry volcano. 'Villain! Villain!'

She put a hand to her mouth. 'You could be right. It could easily carry a villain. Some pirate captain and his cut-throat crew.' She became reminiscent. 'My two favourite authors, you know, when I was young—well, I'd still read them now, if I could—were J. R. R. Tolkien and A. A. Milne. Well, this is more like the *movie* versions, of course, but still ... Oooh! Could they be *rapists* and *slavers*, Argonheart?'

She took his silence for disapproval. 'Not that I really want anything nasty to happen to us. Not really. But it's *thrilling*, isn't it, wondering?'

'I—,' said Argonheart Po. 'I—'

Miss Ming, as she anticipated the occupants of the ship, seemed torn between poles represented in her fantasies by the evil, fascinating Sauron and the soft, jolly Winnie-the-Pooh.

'Will they be fierce, do you think, Argonheart? Or cuddly?' She bit her lower lip. 'Better still, they might be fierce *and* cuddly!'

'Aaaaaah,' breathed Argonheart.

She looked at him in surprise. She appeared to make an effort to retrieve herself from sentiment which, she had doubtless learned, was not always socially acceptable in this world. She achieved the retrieval by a return to her previous alternative, her vein of heavy cynicism. 'I was only joking,' she said.

'Sadist,' hissed Argonheart. 'This might have been deliberately engineered.'

'Well,' she said, having determined her new attitude, 'at least it might be someone to relieve the awful *boredom* of this bloody planet!'

Still bowed, her baffled and grieving escort turned from the blackened fragments of his culinary dreams to stare wistfully after his surviving stegosauri and tyrannosauri which, startled by the ship, were in rapid and uncertain flight in all directions.

His self-control returned. He became a fatalist. His little shrug went virtually unnoticed by her.

'It is fate,' declared the Master Chef. 'At least I am no longer in a dilemma. The decision has been taken from me.'

He began to wade, as best the sticky glue would allow him, towards her.

'Couldn't you round them up?' she asked. 'The ones who survived?'

'And make only a partial contribution? No. I shall find Abu Thaleb and tell him he must create something for himself. A few turns of a power ring, of course, and he will have a feast of sorts, though it will lack the inspiration of anything I could have prepared for him.' A certain guilt, it seemed, inspired him to resent the object of his guilt and therefore made him feel somewhat aggressive towards Abu Thaleb.

He reached Miss Ming's side. 'Shall we return to the party together?'

'But what of the ship?'

'It has done its terrible work.'

'But the people who came in it?'

'I forgive them,' said Argonheart with grandiose magnanimity.

'I mean—don't you want to see what they look like?'

'I bear them no ill-will. They were not aware of the horror they brought. It is ever thus.'

'They might be interesting.'

'*Interesting?*' Argonheart Po was incredulous.

'They might have some news, or something.'

Argonheart Po looked again upon the spaceship. 'They are scarcely likely to be anything but crude, ill-mannered rogues, Miss Ming. Surely, they must have seen, by means of their instruments, my herds?'

'It could be a crash-landing.'

'Perhaps.' Argonheart Po was a fair-minded chef. He did his best to see her point. 'Perhaps.'

'They might need help.'

He cast one final glance about the smoking detritus and said, with not a little violence, 'Well, I hope that they find it.'

'Shouldn't we ... ?'

'I return to find Abu Thaleb and tell him of the disaster.'

'Oh, very well, I suppose I shall have to come with you. But, really, Argonheart, you're looking at this in a rather selfish way, aren't you? This could be a great event. Remember those other aliens who turned up recently? They were trying to help us, too, weren't they? It would be lovely to have some *nice* news for a change ...'

She reached for his arm, so that he might escort her through the glutinous pools.

At that moment there came a grinding noise from the vessel. Both looked back.

A circular section in the hull was turning.

'The airlock,' she gasped. 'It's opening.'

The door of the airlock swung back, apparently on old-fashioned hinges, to reveal a dark hole from which, for a few seconds, flames poured.

'They can't be human,' she said. 'Not if they live in fire.'

No further flames issued from within the ship but from the darkness of the interior there came at intervals tiny flashes of light.

'Like fireflies,' whispered Mavis Ming.

'Or eyes,' said Argonheart, his attention held for the moment.

'The feral eyes of wild invaders.' Miss Ming seemed to be quoting from one of her girlhood texts.

An engine murmured and the ship shivered. Then, from somewhere inside the airlock, a wide band of metal began to emerge.

'A ramp,' said Mavis Ming. 'They're letting down a ramp.'

The ramp slid slowly to the ground, making a bridge between airlock and Earth, but still no occupant emerged.

Mavis cupped her hands around her mouth. 'Greetings!' she cried. 'The peaceful people of Earth welcome you!'

There was still no acknowledgement from the ship. Grainy dust drifted past. There was silence.

'They might be afraid of us,' suggested Mavis.

'Most probably they are ashamed,' said Argonheart Po. 'Too abashed to display themselves.'

'Oh, Argonheart! They probably didn't even see your dinosaurs!'

'Is that an excuse?'

'Well . . .'

Now a muffled, querulous voice sounded from within the airlock, but the language it used was unintelligible.

'We have no translators.' Argonheart Po consulted his power rings. 'I have no means of making him speak any sort of tongue I'll understand. Neither have I the means to understand him. We must go. Lord Jagged of Canaria usually has a translation ring. Or the Duke of Queens. Or Doctor Volospion. Anyone who keeps a menagerie will . . .'

'Sssh,' she said. 'The odd thing is, Argonheart, that while I can't actually understand the words, the language *does* seem familiar. It's like—well, it's like English—the language I used to speak before I came here.'

'You cannot speak it now?'

'Obviously not. I'm speaking this one, whatever it is, aren't I?'

The voice came again. It was high-pitched. It tended to trill, like birdsong, and yet it was human.

'It's not unpleasant,' she said, 'but it's not what I would have called *manly*.' She was kind: 'Still, the pitch might be affected by a change in the atmosphere, mightn't it?'

'Possibly.' Argonheart peered. 'Hm. One of them seems to be coming out.'

At last a space traveller emerged at the top of the ramp.

'Oh, dear,' murmured Miss Ming. 'What a disappointment! I hope they're not all like him.'

Although undoubtedly humanoid, the stranger had a distinctly bird-like air to him. There was a wild crest of bright auburn hair, which rose all around his head and created a kind of ruff about his neck; there was a sharp pointed nose; there were vivid blue eyes which bulged and blinked in the light; there was a head which craned forward on an elongated neck and which would sometimes jerk back a little, like a chicken's as it searched for grain amid the farmyard's dust; there was a tiny body which also moved in rapid, poorly-coordinated jerks and twitches; there were two arms, held stiffly at the sides of the body, like clipped wings. And then there was the plaintive, questioning cry, like a puzzled gull's:

'Eh? Eh? Eh?'

The eyes darted this way and that and then fixed suddenly upon Mavis Ming and Argonheart Po. They received the creature's whole attention.

'Eh?'

He blinked imperiously at them. He trilled a few words.

Argonheart Po waited until the newcomer had finished before announcing gravely:

'You have ruined the Commissar of Bengal's dinner, sir.'

50

'Eh?'

'You have reduced a carefully-planned feast to a rabble of side-dishes!'

'Fallerunnerstanja,' said the visitor from space. He reached back into the airlock and produced a black frock coat dating from a period at least 150 years before Mavis Ming's own. He drew the coat over his shirt and buttoned it all the way down. 'Eh?'

'It's not very clean,' said Mavis, 'that coat. Is it?'

Argonheart had not noticed the stranger's clothes. He was regretting his outburst and trying to recover his composure, his normal amiability.

'Welcome,' he said, 'to the End of Time.'

'Eh?'

The space traveller frowned and consulted a bulky instrument in his right hand. He tapped it, shook it and held it up to his ear.

'Well,' said Mavis with a sniff. '*He* isn't much is he? I wonder if they're all like him.'

'He could be the only one,' suggested Argonheart Po.

'Like that?'

'The only one at all.'

'I hope not!'

As if in response to her criticism the creature waved both his arms in a sort of windmilling motion. It seemed for a moment as if he were trying to fly. Then, with stiff movements, reminiscent of a poorly-controlled marionette, the creature retreated back into its ship.

'Did we frighten him, do you think?' asked Argonheart Po in some concern.

'Quite likely. What a weedy little creep!'

'Mm?'

'What a rotten specimen! He doesn't go with the ship at all. I was expecting someone tanned, brawny, handsome . . .'

'Why so? You know these ships? You have met those who normally use them?'

'Only in my dreams,' she said.

Argonheart made no further effort to follow her. 'He is

51

humanoid, at least. It makes a change, don't you think, Miss Ming, from all those others?'

'Not much of one though.' She shifted a gluey foot. 'Ah, well! Shall we return, as you suggested?'

'You don't think we should remain?'

'There's no point, is there? Let someone else deal with him. Someone who wants a curiosity for their menagerie.'

Argonheart Po offered his arm again. They began to wade towards the dusty shore.

As they reached the higher ground they heard a familiar voice from overhead. They looked up.

Abu Thaleb's howdah hovered there.

'Aha!' said the Commissar of Bengal. His face, with its beard carefully curled and divided into two parts, set with pearls and rubies, after the original, peered over the edge of the air car. 'I thought so.' He addressed another occupant, invisible to their eyes. 'You see, Volospion, I was right.'

'Oh, dear.' Mavis tried to re-arrange her disordered dress. 'Doctor Volospion, too ...'

Volospion's tired tones issued from the howdah. 'Yes, indeed. You were quite right, Abu Thaleb. I apologise. It is a spaceship. Well, if you feel you would like to descend, I shall not object.'

The howdah came down to earth beside Argonheart Po and Miss Ming. Within, it was lined with dark green and blue plush.

Doctor Volospion lay among cushions, still in black and gold, his tight hood covering his skull and framing his pale face. He made no attempt to move. He scarcely acknowledged Miss Ming's presence as he addressed Argonheart Po:

'Forgive this intrusion, great Prince of Pies. The Commissar of Bengal is bent on satisfying his curiosity.'

Argonheart Po made to speak but Abu Thaleb had already begun again:

'What a peculiar odour it has—sweet, yet bitter ...'

'My creations ...' said Argonheart.

'Like death,' pronounced Doctor Volospion.

'The smell is all that is left,' insisted Argonheart now, 'of

52

the dinner I was preparing for your party, Abu Thaleb. The ship's landing destroyed almost all of it.'

Climbing from his howdah the slender Commissar clapped the chef upon his broad back. 'Dear Argonheart, how sad! But another time, I hope, you will be able to recreate all that you have lost today.'

'It is true that there were imperfections,' Argonheart told him, 'and I would relish the opportunity to begin afresh.'

'Soon, soon, soon. What a lovely little ship it is!' Abu Thaleb's plumes bounced upon his turban. 'I had yearnings, you see, to embellish my menagerie, but I fear the ship is too small to accommodate the kind of prize I seek.'

Mavis Ming said: 'You'd be even more disappointed than me, Abu Thaleb. You should see the little squirt we saw just before you turned up. He—'

Doctor Volospion, so it seemed, had not heard her begin to speak. He called from his cushions:

'Your menagerie is already a marvel, Belle of Bengal. The most refined collection in the world. Splendid, specialised, so much more sophisticated than the scrambled skelter of species scraped together by certain so-called connoisseurs whose zoos surpass yours only in size but never in superiority of sensitive selection!'

Mavis Ming displayed confusion. Although Doctor Volospion appeared to address Abu Thaleb he seemed to be speaking for her benefit. She looked from one to the other, wondering if she should form a smile.

Doctor Volospion winked at her.

Mavis grinned. She had been forgiven for her outburst. The joke was at Abu Thaleb's expense.

She began to giggle.

'Go on, Doctor Volospion. I'm sure Abu Thaleb enjoys your flattery,' she said.

'In taste, salutory Commissar, you are assured of supremacy, until our planet passes at last into that limbo of silence and non-existence which must soon, we are told, be its fate.'

Abu Thaleb's back was to Miss Ming and she seemed glad

of this. She held her breath. She went deep red. She made a muted, spluttering noise.

But now the Commissar of Bengal was looking back at Doctor Volospion. 'Oh, really, my friend!' He was good-natured. 'You are capable of subtler mockery than this!'

'But I am a true showman, Abu Thaleb. I relate properly to my audience.'

'Can that be so?' Abu Thaleb turned to Mavis. 'You have seen the visitors, then, Miss Ming?'

'Briefly,' she said. 'Actually, there only seems to be one.'

Abu Thaleb stroked his beard, his pearls and rubies. 'He is not in any way, I suppose, um—elephantoid?'

She was prepared to allow herself a giggle now. She glanced sidelong towards the lounging Volospion.

'Not a trace of a trunk, I'm afraid.' She looked for approval from her protector. 'Not even a touch of a tusk. He couldn't be less like a jumbo, although his nose is long enough, I suppose. He's more like one of those little birds, Abu Thaleb, who pick stuff out of elephant's teeth.'

'Excellent!' applauded Doctor Volospion. 'Ha, ha, ha!'

Abu Thaleb turned and regarded her with mysterious gravity. 'Teeth?'

She giggled again. 'Don't they have teeth, then, anymore?'

Argonheart Po seemed much embarrassed. His glance at Doctor Volospion was almost disapproving. 'I must away to my thoughts,' he said. 'I shall leave this sad scene. There is nothing I can save. Not now. So I'll wish you all farewell.'

'Are we to be denied even a taste of your palatable treasure, Argonheart?' Doctor Volospion used much the same voice as the one he had used to speak to Abu Thaleb. 'Hm?'

Argonheart Po cleared his throat. He shook his head. He glanced at the ground. 'I think so.'

'Oh, but Argonheart, you still have a few dinosaurs left. Can't I see one now? On the horizon.' Miss Ming clutched at his hand but failed to engage.

'No more, no more,' said the Master Chef.

Doctor Volospion spoke again. 'Ah, mighty Lord of the

Larder, how haughty you can sometimes be! Just a morsel of mastadon, perhaps, to whet our appetites?'

'I made no mastadons!' bellowed Argonheart Po, and now he was striding away. 'Good-bye to you!'

Doctor Volospion stirred in his cushion. 'Well, well. Obsessive people can be very poorish sometimes, I think.'

Mavis Ming said: 'He was more interested in his confectionery than any opportunity for contact with another intelligence. Still, he *was* upset.'

'Then you are the only one of us to have tasted his preparations.' Abu Thaleb looked doubtfully at the congealing lake between him and the spaceship.

'How were his dishes, by the by, Miss Ming?' Doctor Volospion wished to know. 'You sampled them, eh?'

Miss Ming adopted something of a worldly air for Doctor Volospion's approval. She uttered a light, amused laugh. 'Oh, a bit over-flavoured, really, if the truth be told.'

His thin tongue ran the line of his lips. 'Too strong, the taste?'

'He's not as good as they say he is, if you ask me. All this'— she rotated a wrist—'all these big ideas.'

Abu Thaleb would not allow such malice. 'Argonheart Po is the greatest culinary genius in the history of the world!'

'Perhaps our world has not been well-favoured with cooks ...' suggested Doctor Volospion slyly.

'And he is the most good-hearted of fellows! The *time* he must have spent preparing the feast for today!'

'Time?' inquired Volospion in some disbelief. 'Time? Time?'

'His presents are famous. Not long since, he made me a savoury mammoth that was the most delicious thing I have ever eaten. An arrangement of flavours defeating description, and yet possessing a unity of taste that was inevitable!' Abu Thaleb was displaying unusual vivacity.

Doctor Volospion was incapable of diplomacy now. He was as one who has hooked his shark and refuses to cut the line, no matter what damage may ensue to both boat and man.

'Perhaps you confuse the subject-matter with the art, admirable Abu?'

Mavis Ming would also take hold of the rod, secure in the approval of her protector, inspired by his wit. 'One man's elephant steak, after all, is another man's bicarbonate of soda!'

And now it was as if rod and line snapped over the side to be borne to the depths.

Abu Thaleb stared at her in frank bewilderment.

Doctor Volospion turned from his prey, his grey face controlled. There was a pause. His expression changed. A secretive smile, for himself more than for her.

The Commissar of Bengal had been saved from conflict and as a result became confused. 'Well,' he said weakly, 'I for one am always astonished by his invention.'

Miss Ming became aware of the atmosphere. Such an atmosphere often followed her funniest observations. 'I'm being too subtle and obscure. I'm sorry. No—Argonheart can be very clever. Very clever indeed. He's very nice. He's always made me feel very much at home. Oh, dear! Do I always manage to spoil things? It can't be me, can it?'

Doctor Volospion, for reasons of his own, had cast a fresh line. 'My dear Miss Ming, you are being too kind again!'

He raised a long hand, the fingers curled forwards to form a claw. 'Do not let this clever Commissar confuse you into compromising your opinions. Be true to your own convictions. If you find Argonheart's work unsatisfactory, not up to the demands of your palate, then say so.'

Abu Thaleb this time ignored the bait. 'Volospion you mock us both too much,' he protested. 'Leave Miss Ming, at least, alone!'

'Oh, he's not mocking *me*,' Miss Ming observed.

'I?' Doctor Volospion moved his brows in apparent astonishment. 'Mock?'

'Yes. Mock.' Abu Thaleb studied the spaceship.

'You do me too much credit, my friend.'

'Hum,' said Abu Thaleb.

Mavis Ming laughed amiably. 'You never know when he's

being serious or when he's joking, do you, Commissar?'

Abu Thaleb was brief. 'Well, Miss Ming, if you are not discomforted, then—'

He was interrupted by Doctor Volospion, who pointed to the ship.

'Ha! Our guest emerges!'

CHAPTER SIX

*In which Mr Emmanuel Bloom Lays Claim to
his Kingdom*

Once more he stood before them, his head bent forwards, his bright blue eyes glittering, his stiff arms at his sides, his red hair flaring to frame his face. He remained for some while at the top of the ramp. He watched them, not with caution but with dispassionate curiosity.

He had changed his clothes.

Now he had on a suit of crumpled black velvet, a shirt whose stiff, high collar rose as if to support his chin, whose cuffs covered his clenched hands to the knuckles. His feet were small and there were tiny, shining pumps on them. He leaned so far over the ramp that he threatened to topple straight down it.

'What an altogether ridiculous figure,' hissed Miss Ming to Doctor Volospion. 'Don't you think?'

She would have said more but, for the moment, she evidently felt the compelling authority of those bulging blue eyes.

'Not from space at all,' complained the Commissar of Bengal. 'He's a time traveller. His clothes . . .'

'Oh, no.' Miss Ming was adamant. 'We saw him arrive. The ship came from space.'

'From the *sky*, perhaps, but not from space.' Abu Thaleb pushed pearls away from his mouth. 'Now—'

But the newcomer had struck a strange pose, arms stiffly extended before him, little mouth smiling, head held up. He spoke in fluting, musical tones that were this time completely comprehensible to them all.

'I welcome you, people of Earth, to my presence. I cannot

58

say how moved I am to be among you again and I appreciate your own feelings on this wonderful day. For the Hero of your greatest legends returns to you. Ah, but how you must have yearned for me. How you must have prayed for me to come back to you! To bring you Life. To bring you Reassurance. To bring you that Tranquillity that can only be achieved by Pain! Well, dear people of Earth, I am back. At long last I am back!'

'Back ... ?' grunted Abu Thaleb.

'Oh, the journey has demented him,' suggested Mavis Ming.

Abu Thaleb cleared his throat. 'I believe you have the advantage, sir ...'

'We missed the name,' explained Doctor Volospion, his voice a fraction animated.

A sweet smile appeared upon the creature's ruby lips. 'But you *must* recognise me!'

'Not a stirring of memory, for my part,' said Doctor Volospion.

'A picture, perhaps, in the old cities. But no ...' said Abu Thaleb.

'You *do* look like someone. Some old writer or other,' said Miss Ming. 'I never did literature.'

He frowned. He turned his palms inwards. He looked down at his strange body. His voice trilled on. 'Yes. Yes. I suppose it is possible that you do not recognise this particular manifestation.'

'Perhaps you could offer a clue.' Doctor Volospion sat up in his cushions for the first time.

He was ignored. The newcomer was patting at his chest. 'I have changed my physical appearance so many times that I have forgotten how I looked at first. The body has probably diminished quite a lot. The hands are certainly of a different shape. Once, as I recall, I was fat. As fat as your friend—ah, he's gone!—the one who was here when I first emerged and whose language I couldn't understand—the tranlator is working fine now, eh? Good, good. Oh, yes! Quite as fat as him. Fatter. And tall, I think, too. Much taller than any of you.

But I leant towards economy. I had the opportunity to change. To be more comfortable in the confines of my ship. I caused my physique to be altered. Irreversibly. This form was modelled after a hero of my own whose name and achievements I forget.' He drew a deep breath. 'Still, the form is immaterial. I am here, as I say, to bring you Fulfilment.'

'I am sure that we are all grateful,' said Doctor Volospion.

'But your name, sir?' Abu Thaleb reminded him.

'Name? Names! Names! Names! I have so many!' He flung back his head and gave forth a warbling laugh. 'Names!'

'Just one would help . . .' said Abu Thaleb without irony.

'Names?' His blue eyes fixed them. He gestured. 'Names? How would you have me called? For I am the Phoenix! I am the Sun's Eagle! I am the Sun's Revenge!' He strutted to the very edge of the ramp but still did not descend. He leaned against the airlock opening. 'You shall know me. You shall! For I am the claws, come to take back the heart you stole from the centre of that great furnace that is my Lord and my Slave. Eh? Do you recall me now, as I remind you of your crimes?'

'Quite mad,' said Miss Ming in a low, tense voice. 'I think we'd better . . .' But her companions were fascinated.

'Here I am!' He spread his legs and arms, to fill the airlock: X. 'Magus, clown and prophet, I—Master of the World! Witness!'

Mavis Ming gasped as flames shot from his finger-tips. Flames danced in his hair. Flames flickered from his nostrils. 'Clownly, kingly, priestly eater and disgorger of fire! Ha!'

He laughed and gestured and balls of flame surrounded him.

'I have no ambiguities, no ambitions—I *am* all things! Man and woman, god and beast, child and ancient—all are compatible and all co-exist in me.'

A huge sheet of fire seemed to engulf the whole ship and then vanish, leaving the newcomer standing there at the airlock, his high voice piping, his blue eyes full of pride.

'I am Mankind! I am the Multiverse! I am Life and Death and Limbo, too. I am Peace, Strife and Equilibrium. I am

60

Damnation and Salvation. I am all that exists. And I am *you*!'

He threw back his little head and began to laugh while the three people stared at him in silent astonishment. For the first time he walked a little way down the ramp, balancing on the balls of his feet, extending his arms at his sides. And he began to sing:

'For I am GOD—and SATAN, too!
'PHOENIX, FAUST and FOOL!
'My MADNESS is DIVINE, and COOL my SENSE!
'I am your DOOM, your PROVIDENCE!'

'We are still, I fear, at a loss ...' murmured Doctor Volospion, but he could not be heard by that singing creature whose attention was suddenly, as if for the first time, on Mavis Ming.

Miss Ming retreated a step or two. 'Oo! What do you think you're looking at, chum!'

He stopped his singing. His features became eager. He bent to regard her.

'Ah! What a *splendid* woman!'

He moved still further down the ramp and he was sighing with pleasure.

'Oh, Madonna of Lust. Ah, my Tigress, my Temptation. Mm! Never have I seen such beauty! But this is Ultimate Femininity!'

'I've had enough,' said Miss Ming severely, and she began to edge away.

He did not follow, but his eyes enchained her. His high, singsong voice became ecstatic.

The visitor watched this process with some contempt. 'What Beauty! Ah—I will bring great wings to beat upon your breast.' His hands clenched at air. 'Tearing talons your talents shall grasp! Claws of blood and sinew shall catch the silver strings of your cool harp! Ha! I'll have you, madam, never fear! Ho! I'll bring your blood to the surface of your skin! Hei! It shall pulse there—in service to my sin!'

'I'm not hanging around,' she said, but she did not move.

The other two watched, forgotten by both, as the strange, mad figure pranced upon his ramp, paying court to the fat, bewildered lady in blue and yellow below.

'You shall be mine, madam. You shall be mine! This is worth all those millenia when I was denied any form of consolation, any sort of human company. I have crossed galaxies and dimensions to find my reward! Now I know my two-fold mission. To save this world and to win this woman!'

'No chance,' she breathed. 'Ugh!' She panted but could not flee.

He ignored her, or else had not heard her, his attention drawn back to Doctor Volospion. 'You asked my name. Now do you recognise me?'

'Not specifically.' Even Doctor Volospion was impressed by the intensity of the newcomer's speech. 'Um—perhaps another clue?'

Bang! A stream of flame had shot from the man's hand and destroyed one of Werther's unfinished mountains.

Boom! The sky darkened and thunder shook the landscape while lightning struck all about them. Chaos swirled around the ship and out of it stared the newcomer's face shouting:

'There! Is that enough to tell you?'

Abu Thaleb demured. 'That was one of a set of mountains manufactured by someone who was hoping ...'

'Manufactured?'

The thunder stopped. The lightning ceased. The sky became clear again.

'Manufactured? You *make* these pathetic landscapes? From *choice*? Pah!'

'There are other things we make ...'

'And what puny conceits! Paint! I use all that is real for *my* canvases. Fire, water, earth and air—and human souls!'

'We can sometimes achieve quite interesting effects,' continued Abu Thaleb manfully, 'by ...'

'Nonsense! Know you this—that I am the Controller of your Destinies! Re-born, I come among you to give you New Life! I offer the Universe!'

'We have had the Universe,' said Doctor Volospion. 'That

is partly why we are in our current predicament. It is all used up.'

'Bah! Well, well, well. So I must take it upon myself again to rescue the race. I shall not betray you—as you have betrayed me in the past. Again I give you the opportunity. Follow me!'

The Commissar of Bengal passed a hand over the gleaming corkscrew curls of his blue-black beard, he tugged at the red Star of India decorating his left ear-lobe; he fingered a feather of his turban.

'Follow you? By Allah, sir, I'm confounded! Follow you? Not a word, I fear. Not a syllable.'

'That is not what I meant.'

'I think,' interposed Doctor Volospion, 'that our visitor regards himself as a prophet—a chosen spokesman for some religion or other. The phrase he uses is more than familiar to me. Doubtless he wishes to convert us to the worship of his God.'

'God? God! God! I am no servant of a Higher Power!' The visitor's neck flashed back in shock. 'Unless, as can fairly be said, I serve myself—and Mankind, of course . . .'

Doctor Volospion casually changed the colour of his robes to dark green and silver, then to crimson and black. He sighed. He became all black.

The visitor watched this process with some contempt. 'What have we here? A jester to my clown?'

Doctor Volospion glanced up. 'Forgive me if I seem unmannerly. I was seeking an appropriate colour for my mood.'

Abu Thaleb was dogged. 'Sir, if you could introduce yourself, perhaps a little more formally . . . ?'

The stranger regarded him through a milder eye, as if giving the Commissar's remark weighty consideration.

'A name? Just one,' coaxed the Lord of All Elephants. 'It might jog our memories, d'you see?'

'I am your Messiah.'

'There!' cried Doctor Volospion, pleased with his earlier interpretation.

The Messiah raised inflexible arms towards the skies. 'I am

63

the Prophet of the Sun! Flamebringer, call me!'

Still more animated, even amused, Doctor Volospion turned his attention away from his cuffs (now of purple lace) to remark: 'The name is not familiar, sir. Where are you from?'

'Earth! I am from Earth!' The prophet gripped the lapels of his velvet coat. 'You must know me. I have given you every hint.'

'But when did you *leave* Earth?' Abu Thaleb put in, intending help, 'Perhaps we are further in your future than you realise. This planet, you see, is millions, billions, of years old. Why, there is every evidence that it would have perished a long time ago—so far as supporting human life was concerned, at any rate—if we had not, with the aid of our great, old cities, maintained it. You could be from a past so distant that no memory remains of you. The cities, of course, do remember a great deal, and it is possible that one of *them* might know you. Or there are time travellers here, like Miss Ming, with better memories of earlier times than even the cities possess. What I am trying to say, sir, is that we are not being deliberately obtuse. We should be only too willing to show you proper respect if we knew who you were and how we should show it. It is on you, the onus, I regret.'

The head jerked from side to side; a curious cockatoo. 'Eh?'

'Name, rank and serial number!' Miss Ming guffawed.

'Eh?'

'We are an ancient and ignorant people,' Abu Thaleb apologised. 'Well, at least, I speak for myself. I am very ancient and extremely ignorant. Except, I should explain, in the matter of elephants, where I am something of an expert.'

'Elephants?'

The stranger's blue eyes glittered. 'So this is what you have become? Dilettantes! Fops! Dandies! Cynics! Quasi-realists!'

'We have become all things at the End of Time,' said Doctor Volospion. 'Variety flourishes, if originality does not.'

'Pah! I call you lifeless bones. But fear not. I am returned to resurrect you. I am Power. I am the forgotten Spirit of

Mankind. I am Possibility.'

'Quite so,' said Doctor Volospion agreeably. 'But I think, sir, that you underestimate the degree of our sophistication.'

'We have really considered the matter quite closely, some of us,' Abu Thaleb wished the stranger to know. 'We are definitely, it seems, doomed.'

'Not now! Not now!' The little man jerked his hand and fire began to roar upon Argonheart Po's cola lake. It was a bright, unlikely red. There was heat.

'Delightful,' murmured Doctor Volospion. 'But if I may demonstrate . . .' He turned a sapphire ring on his right finger. Pale blue clouds formed over the lake. A light rain fell. The fire guttered. It died. 'You will see,' added Doctor Volospion quickly, noting the stranger's expression, 'that we enjoy a certain amount of control over the elements.' He turned another ring. The fire returned.

'I am not here to match conjuring tricks with you, my jackal-eyed friend!' The stranger gestured and a halo of bright flame appeared around his head. He swept his arms about and black clouds filled the sky once more and thunder boomed again; lightning crashed. 'I use my mastery merely to demonstrate my moral purpose.'

Doctor Volospion raised a delighted hand to his mouth. 'I did not realise . . .'

'Well, you shall! You shall know me! I shall awaken the memory dreaming in the forgotten places of your minds. Then, how gladly you will welcome me! For I am Salvation.' He struck a pose and his high, musical voice very nearly sang his next speech:

'Oh, call me Satan, for I am cast down from Heaven! The teeming worlds of the Multiverse have been my domicile till now; but here I am, come back to you, at long last. You do not know me now—but you shall know me soon. I am He for whom you have been waiting. I am the Sun Eagle. Ah, now shall this old world blossom with my fire. For I shall be triumphant, the terrible, intolerant Master of your Globe.'

He paused only for a second to review his audience, his head on one side. Then he filled his lungs and continued with his litany:

'This is my birthright, my duty, my desire. I claim the World. I claim all its denizens as my subjects. I shall instruct you in the glories of the Spirit. You sleep now. You have forgotten how to fly on the wild winds that blow from Heaven and from Hell, for now you cower beneath a mere breeze that is the cold Wind of Limbo. It flattens you, deadens you, and you abase yourselves passively before it, because you know no other wind.'

His hands settled upon his hips. 'But I am the wind. I am the air and the fire to resurrect your Spirit. You two, you bewildered men, shall be my first disciples. And you, woman, shall be my glorious consort.'

Mavis Ming gave a little shudder and confided to Abu Thaleb: 'I couldn't think of anything worse. What a bombastic little idiot! Isn't one of you going to put him in his place?'

'Oh, he is entertaining, you know,' said Abu Thaleb tolerantly.

'Charming,' agreed Doctor Volospion. 'You should be flattered, Miss Ming.'

'What? Because he hasn't seen another woman in a thousand years?'

Doctor Volospion smiled. 'You do yourself discredit.'

The stranger did not seem upset by the lack of immediate effect he had on them. He turned grave, intense eyes upon her. Mavis Ming might have blushed. He spoke with thrilling authority, for all his pre-pubescent pitch:

'Beautiful and proud you may be, woman, yet you shall bend to me when the time comes. You shall not then react with callow cynicism.'

'I think you've got rather old-fashioned ideas about women, my friend,' said Miss Ming staunchly.

'Your true soul is buried now. But I shall reveal it to you.'

The sky began to clear. A flock of transparent pteranadons sailed unsteadily overhead, fleeing the sun. Miss Ming pretended an interest in the flying creatures. But it was plain that the stranger had her attention.

'I am Life,' he said, 'and you are Death.'

66

'Well ...' she began, offended.

He explained: 'At this moment everything is Death that is not me.'

'I'm beginning to pity you,' said Mavis Ming in an artificial voice. 'It's obvious that you've been so long in space, whatever your name is, that you've gone completely mad!' She made nervous tuggings and pullings at her costume. 'And if you're trying to scare me, or turn my stomach, or make fun of me, I can assure you that I've dealt with much tougher customers than you in my time. All right?'

'So,' he said, in tones meant only for her, 'your mind resists me. Your training resists me. Your mother and your father and your society resist me. Perhaps even your body resists me. But your soul does not. Your soul listens. Your soul pines for me. How many years have you refused to listen to its promptings? How many years of discomfort, of sorrow, of depravity and degradation? How many nights have you battled against your dreams and your true desires? Soon you shall kneel before me and know your own power, your own strength.'

Miss Ming took a deep breath. She looked to Doctor Volospion for help, but his expression was bland, mildly curious. Abu Thaleb seemed only embarrassed.

'Listen, you,' she said. 'Where I come from women have had the vote for a hundred and fifty years. They've had equal rights for almost a hundred. There are probably more women in administrative jobs than there are men and more than fifty per cent of all leading politicians are women and when I left we hadn't had a big war for ten years, and we know all about dictators, sexual chauvinists and old-fashioned seducers. I did a History of Sexism course as part of my post-graduate studies, so I know what I'm talking about.'

He listened attentively enough to all this before replying. 'You speak of Rights and Precedents, woman. You refer to Choice and Education. But what if these are the very chains which enslave the spirit? I offer you neither security nor responsibility—save the security of knowing your own identity and the responsibility of maintaining it. I offer you Dignity.'

Miss Ming opened her mouth.

'I note that you are a romantic, sir,' said Doctor Volospion with some relish.

The stranger no longer seemed aware of his presence, but continued to stare at Mavis Ming who frowned and cast about in her troubled skull for appropriate defence. She failed and instead sought the aid of her protector.

'Can we go now?' she whispered to Doctor Volospion. 'He might do something dangerous.'

Doctor Volospion lowered his voice only a trifle. 'If my reading of our friend's character is correct, he shares a preference with all those of his type for words and dramatic but unspecific actions. I find him quite stimulating. You know my interests . . .'

'Do not reject my gifts, woman,' warned the stranger. 'Others have offered you Liberty (if that is what it is) but I offer you nothing less than yourself—your whole self.'

Miss Ming tried to bridle and, unsuccessful, turned away. 'Really, Doctor Volospion,' she began urgently, 'I've had enough . . .'

Abu Thaleb attempted intercession. 'Sir, we have few established customs, though we have enjoyed and continue to enjoy many fashions in manners, but it would seem to me that, since you are a guest in our Age . . .'

'Guest!' The little man was astonished. 'I am not your guest, sir, I am your Saviour.'

'Be that as it may . . .'

'There is no more to be said. There is no question of my calling!'

'Be that as it may, you are disturbing this lady, who is not of our Time and is therefore perhaps more sensitive to your remarks than if she were, um, indigenous to the Age. I think "stress" is the word I seek, though I am not too certain of how "stress" manifests itself. Miss Ming?' He begged for illumination.

'He's a pain in the neck, if that's what you mean,' said Miss Ming boldly. 'But you get used to that here.' She drew herself up.

'As a gentleman, sir—' continued Abu Thaleb.

'Gentleman? I have never claimed to be a "gentleman". Unless by that you mean I am a man—a throbbing, ardent, lover of women—of one woman, now—of *that* woman!' His quivering finger pointed.

Miss Ming turned her back full on him and clambered into Abu Thaleb's howdah. She sat, stiff-necked, upon the cushions, her arms folded in front of her.

The stranger smiled almost tenderly. 'Ah, she is so beautiful! So feminine! Ah!'

'Doctor Volospion,' Miss Ming's voice was flat and cold. 'I should like to go home now.'

Doctor Volospion laughed.

'Nonsense, my dear Miss Ming.' He bowed a fraction to the stranger, as if to apologise. 'It has been an eternity since we entertained such a glorious guest. I am eager to hear his views. You know my interest in ancient religion—my collection, my menagerie, my investigations—well, here we have a genuine prophet.' A deeper bow to the stranger. 'A preacher who shows Li Pao up for the parsimonious hair-splitter that he is. If we are to be berated for our sins, then let it be full-bloodedly, with threats of fire and brimstone!'

'I said nothing of brimstone,' said the stranger.

'Forgive me.'

Miss Ming leaned from the howdah to put her lips to Doctor Volospion's ear. 'You think he's genuine, then?'

He stroked his chin. 'Your meaning is misty, Miss Ming.'

'Oh, I give up,' she said. 'It's all right for everybody else, but that madman's more or less announced his firm decision to rape me at the earliest opportunity.'

'Nonsense,' objected Doctor Volospion. 'He has been nothing but chivalrous.'

'It would be like being raped by a pigeon,' she added. She withdrew into herself.

Doctor Volospion's last glance in her direction was calculating but when he next addressed the stranger he was all hospitality. 'Your own introduction, sir, has been perhaps a mite vague. May I be more specific in my presentation of myself and my friends. This lovely lady, whose beauty has understandably made such an impression upon you, is Miss Mavis Ming. This gentleman is Abu Thaleb, Commissar of Bengal—'

'—and Lord of All Elephants,' modestly appended the Commissar.

'—while I, your humble servant, am called Doctor Volospion. I think we share similar tastes, for I have long studied the religions and the faiths of the past and judge myself something of a connoisseur of Belief. You would be interested, I think, in my collection, and I would greatly value your inspection of it for, in truth, there are few fellow spirits in this world-weary Age of ours.'

The stranger's red lips formed a haughty smile. 'I am no theologian, Doctor Volospion. At least, only in the sense that I am, of course, All Things . . .'

'Of course, of course, but—'

'And I see you for a trickster, a poseur.'

'I assure you—'

'I know you for a poor ghost of a creature, seeking in bad casuistry, to give a dead mind some semblance of life. You are cold, sir, and the cruelties by means of which you attempt to warm your own blood are petty things, the products of a niggardly imagination and some small, but ill-trained, intelligence. Only the generous can be truly cruel, for they know also what it is to be truly charitable.'

'You object to casuistry, and yet you do not disdain the use of empty paradox, I note.' Doctor Volospion remained, so it appeared, in good humour. 'I am sure, sir, when we are better acquainted, you will not be so wary of me.'

'Wary? I should be wary? Ha! If that is how you would misrepresent my nature, to comfort yourself, then I give you full permission. But know this—in giving that permission I am allowing you to remain in the grave when it might have been that you could have known true life again.'

'I am impressed . . .'

'No more! I am your Master, whether you acknowledge it or no, whether I care or no, and that is unquestionable. I'll waste no more energy in debate with you, manikin.'

'Manikin!' Miss Ming snorted. 'That's a good one.'

Doctor Volospion put a finger on his lips. 'Please, Miss Ming. I would continue this conversation.'

'After he's insulted you——'

'He speaks his mind, that is all. He does not know our preferences for euphemism and ornament, and so—'

'Exactly,' said Abu Thaleb, relieved. 'He will come to understand our ways soon.'

'Be certain,' fluted the stranger, 'that it is you who will come to understand my ways. I have no respect for customs, manners, fashions, for I am Bloom the Eternal. I am Bloom, who has experienced all. I am Emmanuel Bloom, whom Time cannot touch, whom space cannot suppress!'

'A name at last,' said Doctor Volospion in apparent delight. 'We greet you, Mr Bloom.'

'That's funny,' said Miss Ming, 'you don't look Jewish.'

CHAPTER SEVEN

*In which Doctor Volospion Becomes Eager to Offer
Mr Bloom his Hospitality*

Mr Emmanuel Bloom seemed for the moment to have lost
interest in them. He stood upon the ramp of his spaceship
and stared beyond Argonheart Po's cola lake (still bearing a
whisp or two of flame) towards the barren horizon. He shook
his head in some despair. 'My poor, poor planet. What have
they made of it in my absence?'

'Do you think we could go now?' complained Miss Ming
to Doctor Volospion and Abu Thaleb. 'If you really want to
see him again you could tell him where to find you.' She had
an inspiration. 'Or invite him to your party, Abu Thaleb,
to make up for what he did to Argonheart's feast!'

'He would be welcome, of course,' said the Commissar
doubtfully.

'His conversation would be refreshing, I think,' said Doctor Volospion. He plucked at his ruff and then, with a motion
of a ring, disposed of it altogether. He was once again in
green and silver, his cap tight about his head, emphasising the
angularity of his white features. 'There are many there who
would respond rather better than can I to the tone of his pronouncements. Werther de Goethe, for instance, with his
special yearning for Sin? Or even Jherek Carnelian, if he is
still with us, with his pursuit of the meaning of morality. Or
Mongrove, who shares something of his monumental millen-
ianalism. Mongrove is back from space, is he not?'

'With his aliens,' Abu Thaleb confirmed.

'Well, then, perhaps you should invite him now, courteous
Commissar?'

'We could tell him that the party was in his honour,' suggested Abu Thaleb. 'That would please him, don't you think? If we humour him ...'

'Can't he hear us?' hissed Miss Ming.

'I think he only listens to us when it interests him to do so,' guessed Doctor Volospion. 'His mind appears on other things at present.'

'This is all very uncomfortable for me,' said Mavis Ming, 'though I suppose I shouldn't complain. Not that there's a lot of point, because nobody ever listens to little Mavis. It's too much to expect, isn't it? But, mark my words, he's going to make trouble for all of us, and especially for me. We shouldn't be wondering about inviting him to parties. We should tell him he's not welcome. We should give him his marching orders. Tell him to leave!'

'It is traditional to welcome all visitors to our world, Miss Ming,' said Abu Thaleb. 'Even the dullest has something to offer and we, in turn, can often offer sanctuary. This Mr Bloom, while I agree with you he seems a little deluded as to his importance to us, must have had many experiences of interest. He has travelled, he tells us, through Time and through space. He has knowledge of numerous different societies. There will be many here who will be glad to meet him. Lord Jagged of Canaria, I am sure—'

'Jagged is gone from us again,' said Volospion somewhat sharply. 'Fled, some say, back into Time—to avoid disaster.'

'Well, there are women, too, who would delight in meeting one so passionate. My Lady Charlotina, Mistress Christia, the Iron Orchid ...'

'They're welcome,' said Mavis Ming 'More than welcome. Though what any woman would see in the little creep I don't know.'

'Once he meets other ladies doubtless his own infatuation for you will subside,' said Abu Thaleb encouragingly. 'As you say, you are probably the first woman he has seen for many a long year and he has had no opportunity to select from all our many, wonderful women one who pleases him even more than you do at present. He is evidently a man of great passion.

One might almost call it elephantine in its grandeur.'

Miss Ming put her chin on her fist.

There was a bang. Pensively, Mr Bloom had blown up the rest of Werther's mountains. He continued to remain with his hands on his hips, contemplating the distance.

'Miss Ming. As a student of history have you any knowledge of Mr Bloom?' Doctor Volospion came and sat next to her in the howdah.

'None,' she said. 'Not even a legend. He must be after my Time.'

'A near-contemporary, I would have thought, judging by his dress.'

'He said himself he'd taken on someone else's appearance. Someone he'd admired.'

'Ah, yes. Another prophet, do you think?'

'From the nineteenth century? Who was there? Karl Marx? Neitzsche? Wagner? Maybe he looks a bit like Wagner. No. Someone like that, though. English? It's just not my period, Doctor Volospion. And religion was never my strong subject. The Middle Ages were my own favourite, because people lived such simpler lives, then. I could get quite nostalgic about the Middle Ages, even now. That's probably why I originally started doing history. When I was a little girl you couldn't get me away from all those stories of brave knights and fair ladies. I guess I was like a lot of kids, but I just hung on to that interest, until I went to university, where I got more interested in the politics, well, that was Betty, really, who was the political nut, you know. But she really had some strong ideas about politics—good ideas. She—'

'But you do not recognise Mr Bloom?'

'You couldn't fail to, could you, once you'd seen him? No. Doctor Volospion, can't you send me home on my own?' pleaded Miss Ming. 'If I had a power ring, even a little one, I could ...'

She had hinted to him before that if she were equipped with a power ring or two she would be less of a nuisance to him. Few time travellers, however, were given the rings which tapped the energy of the old cities, certainly not when, like

Miss Ming, they were comparative newcomers to the End of Time. As Doctor Volospion had explained to her before, there was a certain discipline of mind—or at least a habit of mind—which had to be learned before they could be used. Also they were not one of the artifacts which could be reproduced at will. There was a relatively limited number of them. Miss Ming had never been quite convinced by Doctor Volospion's arguments against her having her own power ring, but there was little she could do save hope that one day he would relent.

'Regretfully ...' He gestured. 'Not yet, Miss Ming.' It was not clear to which of her suggestions he was referring. She allowed her disappointment to show on her plump face.

'Hm,' said Mr Bloom from above, 'it is evident that the entire planet will have to be consumed so that, from the ashes, a purer place may prosper.'

'Mr Bloom!' cried Abu Thaleb. 'I would remind you, sir, that while you are a most honoured guest to our world, you will inconvenience a great many people if you burn them up.'

Bloom blinked as he looked down at Abu Thaleb. 'Oh, they will not die. I shall resurrect them.'

'They are perfectly capable of resurrecting one another, Mr Bloom. That is not my point. You see many of us have embarked on schemes—oh, menageries, collections, creations of various kinds—and if you were to destroy them they would be seriously disappointed. It would be the height of bad manners, don't you think?'

'You have already heard my opinion of manners.'

'But—'

'It is for your own good,' Bloom told him.

'Aha! The authentic voice of the prophet!' cried Doctor Volospion. 'Sir, you must be my guest!'

'You begin to irritate me, Doctor Volospion,' piped Emmanuel Bloom, 'with your constant references to me as a guest. I am not a guest. I am the rightful inheritor of this world, controller of the destinies of all who dwell in it, sole Saviour of your souls.'

'Quite,' apologised Doctor Volospion. 'I should imagine, however, that your spaceship, however grandly furnished and with whatever fine amenities, palls on you as a domicile after so many centuries. Perhaps if you would allow me to put my own humble house at your disposal until a suitable palace— or temple, perhaps—can be built for you, I should be greatly flattered.'

'Your feeble attempts at guile begin to irritate me, Doctor Volospion. I am Emmanuel Bloom.'

'So you have told us ...'

'I am Emmanuel Bloom and I can see into every soul.'

'Naturally. I merely ...'

'And this priestly fawning only makes me despair of you still further. If you would defy me, defy me with some dignity.'

'Mr Bloom, I am simply attempting to make you welcome. Your ideas, your language, your attitudes, they are all decidedly unfashionable now. It was my intention to offer you a dwelling from which you may observe the Age at the End of Time, and make plans for its specific salvation—at your leisure.'

'My plans are simple enough. They can apply to any age. I shall destroy everything. Then I shall create it afresh. Your identity will not only be preserved, it will be fully alive, perhaps for the first time since you were born.'

'Most of us,' Abu Thaleb wished to point out, 'were not actually born at all, Mr Bloom ...'

'That is immaterial. You exist now. I shall help you find yourselves.'

'Most of us are content ...'

'You think you are content. Are you never restless? Do you never wake from slumber recalling a dream of something lost, something finer than anything you have ever experienced before?'

'As a matter of fact I have not slept for many a long year. The fashion died, with most people, even before I became interested in elephants.'

'Do not seek to confuse the issue, Abu Thaleb.'

'Mr Bloom, I *am* confused. I have no wish to have my precious pachyderms destroyed by you. My enthusiasm is at its height. I am sure the same can be said for at least half the

76

population, small though it is, of this planet.'

'I cannot heed you,' said Emmanuel Bloom, feeling in the pockets of his velvet suit. 'You will be grateful when it is done.'

'At least you might canvas the opinion of a few more people, Mr Bloom.' Abu Thaleb begged. 'I mean to say, for all I know most people might think the idea a splendid one! It would make a dramatic change, at least ...'

'And besides,' said Doctor Volospion, 'we certainly have the means to resist you, Mr Bloom, should you begin seriously to discommode us.'

Emmanuel Bloom began to stride up the ramp of his spaceship. 'I am weary of all this. Woman, do you come with me now?'

Miss Ming maintained silence.

'Please reconsider, Mr Bloom,' Doctor Volospion said spiritedly, 'as my guest you would share the roof with many great philosophers and prophets, with messiahs and reformers of every description.'

'It sounds,' piped Mr Bloom, 'like Hell.'

'And there are things you should see. Souvenirs of a million faiths. Miraculous artifacts of every kind.'

Emmanuel Bloom seemed mildly interested. 'Eh?'

'Magical swords, relics, supernatural stones—my collection is justly famous.'

Emmanuel Bloom continued on his way.

'You would, as well as enjoying this fabulous company, be sharing the same roof as Miss Ming, who is another guest of mine,' said Doctor Volospion.

'Miss Ming comes with me. Now.'

'Oh, no I don't,' exclaimed Miss Ming.

'What?' Emmanuel Bloom paused again.

'Miss Ming stays with me,' said Doctor Volospion. 'If you wish to visit her, you may visit her at my dwelling.'

'Oh, don't bother with him!' said Mavis Ming.

'You will come to me, in Time, Mavis Ming,' said Emmanuel Bloom.

'That's the funniest thing I've ever heard,' she told him. She said to Doctor Volospion: 'It's a bit insensitive of you, isn't it, Doctor Volospion, to use me as bait? Why do you want him so badly?'

Doctor Volospion ignored the question.

'You would be very comfortable at Castle Volospion,' he told Mr Bloom. 'Everything you could desire—food, wine, luxurious furniture, women, boys, any animal of your taste . . .'

'I need no luxuries and I desire only one woman. She shall be mine soon enough.'

'It would make Miss Ming happy, I am sure, if you became my g— if you used my house.'

'You are determined, I think, to misunderstand my mission upon this world. I have come to re-fire the Earth, as its Leader and its Hero. To restore Love and Madness and Idealism to their proper eminence. To infuse your blood with the stuff that makes it race, that makes the heart beat and the head swim! Look about you, manikin, and tell me if you see any heroes. You no longer have heroes—and you have such paltry villains!'

'It does not seem reasonable of you to judge by we three alone,' said Abu Thaleb.

'Three's enough. Enough to tell the general condition of the whole. Your society is revealed in your language, your gestures, your costumes, your landscapes! Oh, how sad, how ruined, how unfulfilled you are! Ah, how you must have longed, in your secret thoughts, those thoughts hidden even from yourselves, for me to return. And look now—you still do not realise it.'

He smiled benevolently down on them, standing near the entrance to his ship.

'But that realisation shall dawn anon, be sure of that. You ask me to live in one of your houses—in a tomb, I say. And could I bear to leave my ship behind? My much-named ship, the *Golden Hind*? Or *Firedrake* call her, or *Virgin Flame—Pi-meson* or the *Magdelaine*—sailing out of Carthage, Tyre, Old Bristol or Bombay: Captain Emmanual Bloom, late of Jerusalem, founder of the Mayan faith, builder of pyramids, called Ra or Raleigh, dependant on your taste—Kubla Khan or Prester John, Baldur, Mithras, Zoroaster—the Sun's Fool,

78

for I bring you Flame in which to drown! I am blooming Bloom, blunderer through the million planes—I am Bloom, the booming drum of destiny. I am Bloom—the Fireclown! Aha! Now you know me!'

The three faces stared blankly up.

He leaned with his hand against the entrance to the airlock, his head on his shoulder, his eye beady and intelligent. 'Eh?'

Doctor Volospion remained uncharacteristically placatory. 'Perhaps you could enlighten us over a meal? You must be hungry. We can offer the choicest foods, to suit the most demanding of tastes. Please, Mr Bloom, I ask again that you reconsider ...'

'No.'

'You feel I have misinterpreted you, I know. But I am an earnest student. I remain a mite confused. Your penchant for metaphor ...'

The Fireclown clapped a tiny hand to a tiny knee. He frowned at Doctor Volospion. 'One metaphor is worth a million of your euphemisms, Doctor Volospion. I have problems to consider and must seek solitude. I have poetry to write—or to recall—I forget which—and need time for meditation. I should accept your invitation for it is my duty to broaden your mind—but that duty can wait.'

He turned again to regard the woman.

'You'll join me now, Miss Ming?'

His huge blue eyes flashed suddenly with an intelligence, a humour, which shocked her completely from her hard-won composure.

'What?' The response was mindless.

He stretched out a hand. 'Come with me now. I offer you pain and knowledge, lust and freedom. Hm?'

She began to rise, as if mesmerised. She seemed to be shivering. Then she sat down. 'Certainly not!'

Emmanuel Bloom laughed. 'You'll come.' He returned his attention to Doctor Volospion. 'And I would advise you, sir, to save your breath in this meaningless and puny Temptation. Your hatred of me is patent, whether you admit it to yourself or not. I would warn you to cease your irritation.'

'You still refuse to believe my good faith, Mr Bloom. So be it.' Doctor Volospion bowed low.

The ramp was withdrawn. The airlock shut.

No further sound escaped the ship.

CHAPTER EIGHT

*In Which Miss Ming Begins to Feel a Certain
Curiosity Concerning the
Intentions of Emmanuel Bloom*

If anyone at the End of Time expected Mr Bloom to begin immediately to exercise his particular plans for bringing Salvation to the planet they were to be disappointed, for his extravagant spaceship (which the fashion of the moment declared to be in hideous taste) remained where it landed and Emmanuel Bloom, the Fireclown, did not re-emerge. A few sightseers came to view the ship—the usual sensation-seekers like the Duke of Queens (who wanted to put the ship at once into his collection of ancient flying machines), My Lady Charlotina of Below the Lake, O'Kala Incarnadine, Sweet Orb Mace, the Iron Orchid, Bishop Castle and their various followers, imitators and hangers-on—but in spite of all sorts of hallooings, bangings, catcalls, lettings off of fireworks, obscene displays (on the part of the ladies who were curious to see what Miss Ming's most ardent suitor really looked like) and the rest, the great Saviour of Mankind refused to reveal himself; nothing occurred which could be interpreted as action on the Fireclown's part. No fires swept the Earth, no thunders or lightnings broke the calm of the skies, there was no destruction of artifacts nor any further demolition of landscapes. Indeed, it was singularly peaceful, even for the End of Time, and certain people became almost resentful of Mr Bloom's refusal to attempt, at least, a miracle or two.

'Doctor Volospion exaggerated!' pronounced My Lady Charlotina, all in blue and sage, the colours of dreams, as she lunched on a green and recently constructed hillside overlooking the ship (it now stood in clouds of daisies, a memento of the Duke of Queens' pastoral phase which had lasted scarcely the equivalent of an ancient Earth Summer) and raised a turnip (another memento) to her ethereal lips. 'You know his obsessions, my dear O'Kala. His taste for monks and gurus and the like.'

O'Kala Incarnadine, currently a gigantic fieldmouse, nibbled at the lemon he held in both front paws. 'I am not familiar with the creatures,' he said.

'They are not creatures, exactly. They are a kind of person. Lord Jagged was good enough to inform me about them, although, of course, I have forgotten most of what he said. My point is, O'Kala, that Doctor Volospion *wished* this Mr Bloom to be like a guru and so interpreted his words accordingly.'

'But Miss Ming confirmed . . .'

'Miss Ming!'

O'Kala shrugged his mousy shoulders in assent.

'Miss Ming's bias was blatant. Who could express such excessive ardour of anyone, let alone Miss Ming?' My Lady Charlotina wiped the white juice of the turnip from her chin.

'Jherek—he pursues his Amelia with much the same enthusiasm.'

'Amelia is an Ideal—she is slender, beautiful, unattainable —everything an Ideal should be. There is nothing unseemly in Jherek's passion for such a woman.' My Lady Charlotina was unaware of anything contradictory in her remarks. After her brief experience in the Dawn Age she had developed a taste for propriety which had not yet altogether vanished.

'In certain guises,' timidly offered O'Kala, 'I have lusted for Miss Ming myself, so . . .'

'That is quite different. But this Mr Bloom is a *man*.'

'Abu Thaleb's tale was not dissimilar to Doctor Volospion's.'

'Abu Thaleb is impressionable. On elephants he is unequalled, but he is no expert on prophets.'

'Is anyone?'

'Lord Jagged. That is why Doctor Volospion apes him. You

know of the great rivalry Volospion feels for Lord Jagged, surely? For some reason, he identifies with Jagged. Once he used to emulate him in everything, or sought to. Jagged showed no interest. Gave no praise. Since then—oh, so long ago my memory barely grants me the bones of it—Doctor Volospion has set himself up as a sort of contra-Jagged. There are rumours—no more than that, for you know how secretive Jagged can be—rumours of a sexual desire which flourished between them for a while, until Jagged tired of it. Now that Lord Jagged has disappeared, I suspect that Doctor Volospion would take his place in our society, for Jagged has the knack of making us all curious about his activities. You have my opinion in a nutshell—Volospion makes much of this Bloom in an effort to pique our interest, to gossip about him in lieu of Jagged.'

O'Kala Incarnadine wiped his whiskers. 'Then he has succeeded.'

'For the moment, I grant you, but unsubtly. It will not last.'

My Lady Charlotina sighed and sucked at a celery stalk, letting her gaze wander to the scarlet spaceship. 'Our curiosity is still with Jagged. Where can he be? This,' she indicated the vessel with her vegetable, 'is no more than a diversion.'

'It would be amusing, though, if Mr Bloom did begin to lay waste the world.'

'There is no logic to it. The world will be finished soon enough, as everyone knows. The very Universe in which our planet hangs is on the point of vanishing forever. Mr Bloom has brought his salvation at altogether the wrong moment and at a time when salvation itself is unfashionable, even as a topic of conversation.'

'The reasons are obvious ...' began O'Kala, in a rare and philosophical mood, '... for who would wish to discuss such matters, now that we know—?'

'Quite.' My Lady Charlotina waved. An air car was approaching. It was the shape of a great winged man, its bronze head flashing in the red light of the sun, its blind eyes glaring, its twisted mouth roaring as if in agony. The Duke of Queens had modelled his latest car after some image recently discovered by him in one of the rotting cities.

The car landed nearby and from it trooped many of My Lady Charlotina's most intimate friends. From his saddle behind the head of the winged man the Duke of Queens raised his hand in a salute. He had on an ancient astronaut's jacket, in silver-tipped black fur, puffed pantaloons of mauve and ivory stripes, knee-boots of orange lurex hide, a broad-brimmed hat of panda ears, all sewn together in the most fanciful way.

'My Lady Charlotina! We saw you and had to greet you. We are on our way to enjoy the new boys Florence Fawkes had made for her latest entertainment. Will you come with us?'

'Perhaps, but boys . . .' She lifted a corner of her mouth.

My Lady Charlotina noted that Doctor Volospion and Mavis Ming were among those pouring from the body of the winged man. She greeted Sweet Orb Mace with a small kiss, laid a sincere hand upon the arm of Bishop Castle, winked at Mistress Christia and smiled charmingly at Miss Ming.

'Aha! The beauty for whom Mr Bloom crossed the galaxies. Miss Ming, you are the focus of all our envy!'

'Have you seen Mr Bloom?' asked Miss Ming.

'Not yet, not yet.'

'Then wait before you envy me,' she said.

Doctor Volospion's cunning eye glittered. 'There is nothing more certain to attract the attention of a lady to a gentleman, even in these weary times of ours, than the passion of that gentleman for another lady.'

'How perceptive you are, dear Doctor Volospion! It must be admitted. In fact, I believe I already admitted it, when I first greeted you.'

Doctor Volospion bowed his head.

'You are looking at your best,' she continued, for it was true. 'You are always elegant Doctor Volospion.' He had on a long, full-sleeved robe of bottle-green, trimmed with mellow gold, the neck high, to frame his sharp face, a matching tight-fitting cap upon his head, buttoned beneath the pointed chin.

'You are kind, My lady Charlotina.'

'Ever truthful, Doctor Volospion.' She gave her attention to

Miss Ming's white frills. 'And this dress. You must feel so much younger in it.'

'Much,' agreed Miss Ming. 'How clever of you to understand what it was to be like me! How many hundreds of years can it have been?'

'More than that, Miss Ming. Thousands, almost certainly. I see, at any rate, that your would-be ravisher has yet to come out of his little lair again.'

'He can stay there forever as far as I'm concerned.'

'I have made one or two attempts to rouse him,' said Doctor Volospion. 'I sought to shift the ship, too, but it is protected now by a singularly intractable force-field. Nothing I possess can dissipate that field.'

'So he does have the power he boasted of, eh?' Bishop Castle in his familiar tall *tête* which cast a shadow over half the company, looked without much interest at the spaceship.

'Apparently,' said Doctor Volospion.

'But why doesn't he *use* it?' The Duke of Queens joined them. 'Has he perished in there, do you think. In his own mad flames?'

'We should have smelled something, at least,' said O'Kala Incarnadine.

'Well,' Sweet Orb Mace was now a pretty blonde in a black sari, '*you* would have smelled something, O'Kala, with your nose.'

O'Kala wrinkled his current one.

'He's playing cat and mouse with me, that's what I think,' said Mavis Ming with a nervous glance at the vessel. 'Oh, I'm sorry O'Kala, I didn't mean to suggest ...'

O'Kala Incarnadine made a toothy grin. 'I pity any ordinary cat who met a mouse like me!'

'He's hoping I'll give in and go to him. That's typical of some men, isn't it? Well, I had enough of crawling with Donny Stevens. Never again I told my friend Betty. And never again it was!'

'But you have been tempted, eh?' My Lady Charlotina became intimate.

'Not once.'

My Lady Charlotina let disappointment show.

'I wish,' said Mavis Ming, 'that he'd either start something or else just go away. It must have been weeks and weeks he's been waiting there! It's getting on my nerves, you know.'

'Of course, it must be, my dear,' said Sweet Orb Mace.

'Well,' the Duke of Queens reminded them all, 'Florence Fawkes awaits us. Will you come My Lady Charlotina? O'Kala?'

'I have a project,' said My Lady Charlotina, by way of an excuse, 'to finish. Of course, it is very hard to tell if it is properly finished or not. An invisible city populated with invisible androids. You must come and feel it soon.'

'A lovely notion,' said Bishop Castle. 'Are the androids of all sexes?'

'All.'

'And it is possible to—?'

'Absolutely possible.'

'It would be interesting—'

'It is.'

'Aha!' Bishop Castle tilted his *tête*. 'Then I look forward to visiting you at the earliest chance, My Lady Charlotina. What entertainments you do invent for us!' He bowed, almost toppled by his headgear.

The Duke of Queens had resumed his saddle. 'All aboard!' he cried enthusiastically.

It was then that there came a squeak from the space vessel below. The airlock opened. All heads turned.

Emmanuel Bloom's bright-blue eyes regarded them. His high-pitched voice drifted up to them.

'So you have come to me,' he said.

'I?' said the Duke of Queens in astonishment.

'I have waited,' Emmanuel Bloom said, 'for you, Miss Ming. So that you may share my joy.'

Miss Ming drew back into the main part of the gathering. 'I was only passing . . .' she began.

'Come.' He extended a stiff hand from the interior of the ship. 'Come.'

'Certainly not!' She hid behind Doctor Volospion.

'So, the one with the jackal eyes holds you still. And against your will, I am sure.'

'Nothing of the sort! Doctor Volospion is my host, that is all.'

'You are too afraid to tell me the truth.'

'She speaks the truth, sir,' said Volospion in an off-hand tone. 'She is free to come and go from my house as she pleases.'

'Some pathetic enchantment, no doubt, keeps her there. Well, woman, never fear. The moment I know that you need me I shall rescue you, wherever you may be hidden.'

'I don't *need* rescuing,' declared Miss Ming.

'Oh, but you do. So badly do you need it that you dare not tell yourself!'

My Lady Charlotina cried: 'Excuse me, sir, for intruding, but we were wondering if your plans for the destruction of the world were completely formulated. I, for one, would appreciate a little notice.'

'My meditations are not yet completed,' he told her. He still stared at Miss Ming. 'Will you come to me now?'

'Never!'

'Remember my oath.'

Doctor Volospion stepped forward. 'I would remind you, sir, that this lady is under my protection. Should you make any further attempt to annoy her then I must warn you that I shall defend her to the death!'

Miss Ming was taken aback by this sudden about-face. 'Oh, Doctor Volospion! How *noble*!'

'What's this?' said Bloom, blinking rapidly, 'More posturing?'

'I give fair warning, that is all.'

Doctor Volospion folded his arms across his chest and stared full into the eyes of Emmanuel Bloom.

Bloom remained unimpressed. 'So you do keep her prisoner, as I suspected. She believes she has her liberty, but you know better!'

'I shall accept no more insults.' Doctor Volospion lifted his chin in defiance.

'This is not mere braggadocio, I can tell. It is calculated. But what do you plan?'

'Any more of this, sir,' said Doctor Volospion in ringing tones, 'and I shall have to demand satisfaction of you.'

The Fireclown laughed. 'I shall free the woman soon.'

The airlock shut with a click.

'How extraordinary!' murmured My Lady Charlotina. 'How exceptional of you, Doctor Volospion! Miss Ming must feel quite moved by your defence of her.'

'I am, I am.' Miss Ming's small eyes were shining. 'Doctor Volospion. I never *knew* ...'

Doctor Volospion strode for the air car. 'Let us leave this wretched place.'

Miss Ming tripped behind him. It was as if she had found her True Knight at last.

CHAPTER NINE

In which the Fireclown Brings some Small Salvation to the End of Time

It was, as it happened, My Lady Charlotina who first experienced the fiery wrath of Emmanuel Bloom.

Tiring (for reasons described elsewhere) of her apartments under Lake Billy the Kid, she had begun a new palace which was to be constructed in an arrangement of clouds above the site of the lake, so that it hovered over the water, reflecting both this and the sun. It was to be primarily white but with some other pale colours here and there, perhaps for flanking towers. She had spent considerable thought upon the palace and it was still by no means complete, for My Lady Charlotina was not one of those who could create a complete conception with the mere twist of a power ring; she must consider, she must alter, she must build piece by piece. Thus, in the clouds over Lake Billy the Kid, there were half-raised towers, towers without tops, domes with spires and domes that were turretted; there were gaps where halls had been, there were whole patches of space representing apartments which, at a whim, she had returned to their original particles.

After resting, My Lady Charlotina emerged from Lake Billy the Kid and stood upon the shore, surrounded by comfortable oaks and cypresses. She arranged the mist upon the water into more satisfactory configurations, making it drift so high that it mingled with the clouds on which her new palace was settled, and she was about to eradicate a tower which offended, now, her sense of symmetry, when there came a loud roaring sound and the whole edifice burst into flame.

My Lady Charlotina gasped with indignation. Her first

thought was that one of her friends had misjudged an experiment and accidentally set fire to her palace, but she soon guessed the true cause of the blaze.

'The lunatic incendiary!' she cried, and she flung herself into the sky, not to go to her crackling palace (which was beyond salvaging) but to look down upon the world and discover the whereabouts of the Fireclown.

He was not a mile from the conflagration, standing on top of a great plinth meant to support a statue of himself which the Duke of Queens had never bothered to complete. He wore his black velvet, his bow tie, his shirt with its ruffles. He rested upon the plinth like a parrot upon its pedestal, shifting from side to side and flapping his arms at his sides as he studied his handiwork. He did not see My Lady Charlotina as, in golden gauze, she fluttered down towards him.

She paused, to hover a few feet above his head, she waited, watching him, until he became aware of her presence. She listened to him as he spoke to himself.

'Quite good. A fitting symbol. It will look well in any legends, I think. It is best for the first few miracles to be spectacular and not directed at individuals. I should not leave it too late, however, before rescuing the remains of any residents and resurrecting them.'

She could not contain herself.

'I sir, might have been the only resident of that castle in the clouds. Happily, I had not arrived at it before you began your fire-raising!'

His little head jerked here and there. At last he looked up. 'So!'

'The palace was to be my new home, Mr Bloom. It was impolite of you to destroy it.'

'There were no inhabitants?'

'Not yet.'

'Well, then, I shall be on my way.'

'You make no attempt to apologise?'

Mr Bloom was amused. 'I can scarcely apologise for something so calculating. You ask me to lie? I am the Fireclown. Why should I lie?'

She was speechless. Mr Bloom began to climb down a ladder he had placed against the plinth. 'I bid you good morning, madam.'

'Good *morning*?'

'Or good afternoon—you keep no proper hours on this planet at all. It is hard to know. That will be changed,' he smiled, 'in Time.'

'Mr Bloom, your purposes here are quite without point. Are we to be impressed by such displays?' She waved her hand towards the blazing palace. Her clouds had turned brown at the edges. 'Time, Mr Bloom is not what it was. Times, Mr Bloom, have changed since those primitive Dawn Ages when such "miracles" might have provoked interest, even surprise, in the inhabitants of this world. Watch!' She turned a power ring. The fire vanished. An entire, if uninspired, fairy palace glittered again in pristine clouds.

'Hum,' said Mr Bloom, still on his ladder. He began to climb back to the top of the plinth. 'I see. So Volospion is not the only conjurer here.'

'We all have that power. Or most of us. It is our birthright.'

'Birthright? What of my birthright?'

'You have one?'

'It is the world. I explained to Doctor Volospion, madam . . .' He was aggrieved. 'Did he speak to no one of my mission here?'

'He told us what you had said, yes.'

'And you are not yet spiritually prepared, it seems. I left you plenty of time for contemplation of your fate. It is the accepted method, where Salvation is to be achieved.'

'We have no need of Salvation, Mr Bloom. We are immortal, we control the Universe—what's left of it—we are, most of us, without fear (if I understand the term properly).' My Lady Charlotina was making an untypical effort to meet Emmanuel Bloom halfway. It was probably because she had no strong wish to be at odds with him, since she was curious to know better the man who courted Miss Ming with such determination. 'Really, Mr Bloom, you have arrived too late.

Even a few hundred years ago, before we heard of the dissolution of the Universe, there might have been some enjoyment for all, but not now. Not now, Mr Bloom.'

'Hum.' He frowned. He lifted a hand to his face and appeared to peck at his cuff. 'But I have no other role, you see. I am a Saviour. It is all I can do.'

'Must you save a whole world? Aren't there a few individuals you could concentrate on?'

'It hardly seems worth while. I am, to be more specific, a World Saviour—a Saver of Worlds. I have ranged the Multiverse saving them. From all sorts of things, physical and spiritual. And I always leave the places that I have saved spiritually regenerated. Ask any of them. They will all tell you the same. I am loved throughout the teeming dimensions.'

'Then perhaps you could find another world . . .'

'No, this is the last. I left it long ago, promising that I would return and save it, as my final action.'

'Well, you are too late.'

'Really, madam, I cannot take your word for it. I am the greatest authority on such matters in the Universe, to say the least. I am the Champion Eternal, Hero of a million legends. When Law battles Chaos, I am always called. When civilisations are threatened with total extermination, it is to me that they turn for rescue. And when decadence and despair rule an otherwise secure and prosperous world, it is for Emmanuel Bloom, the Fireclown, Time's Jester, that they yearn. And I come.'

'But we did not call you, we require no rescuing. We are not yearning, I assure you, even a fraction.'

'Miss Ming is yearning.'

'Miss Ming's yearning is hardly spiritual.'

'So you think. I know better.'

'Well, then, I'll grant you that Miss Ming is yearning. But I am not yearning. Doctor Volospion is incapable, I am sure, of yearning. Yearning, all in all, Mr Bloom, is extinct in this Age.'

'Forgotten, hidden, unheeded, but I know it is there. I know. A deep, unadmitted sadness. A demand for Romance. A pining for Ideals.'

'We take up Romance from time to time, and we have an interest, on occasion, in Ideals—but these are passing enthusiasms, Mr Bloom. Even those of us most obsessed with such things show no particular misery when circumstances or changing fashion require that they be dropped.'

'How shallow are those who dwell here now! All, that is, save Mavis Ming.'

'Some think her the shallowest of us all.' My Lady Charlotina regretted her spite, for she did not wish to seem malicious in Mr Bloom's eyes.

'It is often the case,' he said. 'With those who cannot see beyond flesh and into the soul.'

'I doubt if there are many souls remaining among us,' said My Lady Charlotina. 'Since we are almost every one of us self-made creatures. There is even some speculation that we are not human at all, but sophisticated androids.'

'It could be the explanation,' he mused.

'I hope you will not be wholly frustrated,' she said sympathetically, watching him climb down his ladder. 'I can imagine what it is like to possess only one role.'

She settled, like a butterfly, upon the vacated plinth.

He reached the ground and peered up at her, arms held stiffly, as usual, by his side, red hair flaring. 'I assure you, madam,' he piped, 'that I am not in the least impressed by what you have told me.'

'But I speak the truth.'

'Unlike Volospion, who lies, lies, lies. I agree that you believe, as does Miss Ming, that you speak the truth. But I see decadence. And where there is decadence, there is misery. And where there is misery, then must come the Fireclown, to bring laughter, joy, terror, to banish all anxieties.'

'Your logic is, I fear obsolete, Mr Bloom. There is no misery here, to speak of. And,' she added, 'there is no joy. Instead, we have a comfortable balance. It enables us to contemplate our own end with a certain grace.'

'Hum.'

'Surely, this equilibrium is what all human morality and philosophy has striven for over the millenia?' she said, seating herself on the edge of the plinth and arranging her gold gauze about her legs. 'Would you set the see-saw swinging again?'

He frowned. 'No heights or depths here, eh?'

'For most of us, no.'

'No Heaven and Hell?'

'Only those we create for our own amusement.'

'No terror and no Ecstasy?'

'Scarcely a scrap.'

'How can you bear it?'

'It is the ultimate achievement of our race. We enjoy it.'

'Are there none who—?'

'Those time travellers, space travellers, a few who have induced special anachronistic tendencies in themselves. Yes, there are some who might respond to you. A good few of them are not with us at present, however. The Iron Orchid's little son, Jherek Carnelian, his great love Amelia Underwood, his mentor Lord Jagged of Canaria and perhaps a few others, one loses track. Doctor Volospion? Perhaps, for it is rumoured that he is not of this Age at all. Li Pao and various aliens who have visited us and stayed ... Yes, from these you could derive a certain satisfaction. Some would undoubtedly welcome you, for one reason or another ...'

'It is usually for one reason or another,' said the Fireclown frankly. 'Men see me as many things. It is because I *am* many things.'

'And all of them excellent, I am sure.'

'But I must do what I must do,' he said. 'It is all I know. For I am Bloom the Destroyer, Bloom the Builder, Bloom the Bringer of Brightness, Bloom who Blooms Forever! And my mission is to save you all.'

'I thought we had at least removed ourselves from generalities, Mr Bloom,' she said a little chidingly.

He turned away disconsolately, so My Lady Charlotina thought.

'Generalities, madam, are all I deal in. They are my stock in trade. It is the gift I bring—to remove petty anxieties, momentary considerations, and to replace them with grandeur, with huge, simple, glorious Ideals.'

'It is not a simple problem,' she said. 'I can see that.'

'It must be a *simple* problem!' he complained. 'All problems are simple. All!'

He disappeared into the soft trees surrounding the plinth. She heard his voice muttering for some while, but he made no formal farewell, for he was too much lost in his own concerns. A short time later she saw a distant tree burst into flame and subside almost at once. She saw a rather feeble bolt of lightning crash and split a trunk. Then he was gone away.

My Lady Charlotina remained on the plinth, for she was enjoying a rare sense of melancholy and was reluctant to let the mood pass.

CHAPTER TEN

*In which the Fireclown Attempts to Deny any
Suggestion so far Made that He is an
Anachronism*

My Lady Charlotina's words had failed, as was soon to be shown, to convince Mr Bloom. Yet there was something pathetic in his acts of destruction, something almost sad about the way he demolished the Duke of Queens' *City of Tulips* (each dwelling a separate flower) or laid waste Florence Fawkes' delightful little *Sodom* with all its inhabitants, including Florence Fawkes who was never, due to an oversight, resurrected. It was in a half-abstracted mood that he brought a rain of molten lava to disrupt the party which Bishop Castle was giving for moody Werther de Goethe (and which, as it happened, was received with approval by all concerned, since Werther was one of the few to appreciate the Fireclown's point of view and died screaming of repentance and the like. Though when he was resurrected, almost immediately, he did complain that the consistency of the lava was not all that it might have been—too lumpy, he thought). The Fireclown rarely appeared personally on any of these occasions. He seemed to have lost the will to enjoy intercourse with his fellows. Moreover, there was scarcely anyone who found him very entertaining, after the first demolition or two, largely because his wrath always took exactly the same form. Werther de Goethe sought him out and enthused. He found, he said, Mr Bloom deeply refreshing, and he offered himself as an acolyte. Mr Bloom had informed him that he would let Werther know when acolytes were needed, if at all. Lord Mongrove also visited the Fireclown, hoping for conversation,

96

but the Fireclown told him frankly that his talk was depressing. My Lady Charlotina visited him, too, and came away refusing to tell anyone what had passed between herself and Mr Bloom, though she seemed upset. And when Mistress Christia followed close in the footsteps of her friend and was also rebuffed, Mr Bloom told her sombrely that he waited for one woman and one alone—the beautiful Mavis Ming.

Upon hearing this, Miss Ming shuddered and suggested that someone destroy the Fireclown before he did any more damage to the world.

If it had not been for the immense and unshakeable force-field around the Fireclown's ship, there is no doubt that some of the denizens at the End of Time would have at least made an attempt to halt the Fireclown's inconveniencing activities. It was of a type unfamiliar even to the rotting cities, who did their best to analyse it and produce a formula for coping with it, but failed, forgetting the purpose of half their experiments before they were completed and drawing no conclusions from those they did complete, for the same reason. In most cases they took a childish delight in the more spectacular effects of their experiments and would play with the energies they had created until growing tired and petty they refused to help any further.

The Fireclown had been unable to bring quite the holocaust he had promised, for things were rebuilt as soon as he had destroyed them, but he had at least become a large flea upon the flanks of society, wrecking carefully-planned picnics, entertainments, artistic creations and games, so that precautions had to be taken against him which spoiled the general effect intended. Force-fields had to be produced to protect property for the first time in untold thousands of years and even the Duke of Queens, that most charitable of immortals, agreed that his ordinary enjoyment of life was being detrimentally influenced by Mr Bloom, particularly since the destruction of his menagerie, the resurrection of which had greatly discommoded him.

There came such a twittering of protest as had never been heard at the End of Time and plans were discussed interminably for the ridding of the world of this pest. Deputations were sent to his ship and were ignored, polite notes left at his airlock's entrance were either burned on the spot or allowed to drift away on the wind.

'It is quite ridiculous,' said My Lady Charlotina, 'that this puny prophet should be allowed to figure so largely in our lives. If only Lord Jagged were here, he would surely find a solution.'

She spoke spitefully, for she knew that Doctor Volospion was in earshot. They were both attending the same reception, given on Sweet Orb Mace's new lawns which surrounded his mansion, modelled on one of the baroque juvenile slaughter-houses of the late 200,006th century. From within sounded the most authentic screams, causing all to compliment Sweet Orb Mace on an unprecedented, for her, effort of imagination.

'Lord Jagged has undoubtedly found that his interests are not best served by remaining at the End of Time,' said Doctor Volospion from behind her.

She pretended surprise. 'How do you do, Doctor Volospion?' She inspected his costume—another long-sleeved robe, this one of maroon and white. 'Hm.'

'I am well, My Lady Charlotina.'

'The Fireclown has made no attack upon you, yet? That is strange. Of all of us, it is you whom he actually appears to dislike.'

Doctor Volospion lowered his eyes and smiled. 'He would not harm Miss Ming, my guest.'

'Of course!'

She swept silky skirts of brown and blue about her and made to move on, but Volospion stayed her. 'I gather there has been much debate about this Fireclown.'

'Far too much.'

'He would be a marvellous prize for my menagerie.'

'So that is why he mistrusts you!'

'I think not. It is because my logic defeats him.'

'I did not know.'

'Yes. I have probably had the longest debate of anyone at the End of Time with Bloom. He found that he could not best me in argument. It is sheer revenge, the rest. Or so I suspect.'

'Aha?' My Lady Charlotina turned her fine and scented head so that she could smile pleasantly upon the Duke of Queens, strutting past in living koalas. 'Then surely you can conceive a means of halting his activities, Doctor Volospion?'

'I believe that I have done so, madam.'

She laughed, almost rudely. 'But you decide to keep it to yourself.'

'The Fireclown has a certain sensitivity. For all I know he has the means to overhear us.'

'I should not have thought that, temperamentally, he was an ordinary eavesdropper.'

'But I feel, none the less, that I should be cautious.'

'So you'll not illuminate me?'

'To my regret.'

'Well, I wish you luck with your plan, Doctor Volospion.' She looked here and there. 'Where is your guest, the Fireclown's quarry? Where is Miss Ming?'

He expressed secret glee. 'Not here.'

'Not here? She travels to meet her suitor at last?'

'No. On the contrary . . .'

'Then what?' My Lady Charlotina expressed cool impatience.

'Wait,' said Doctor Volospion. 'I protect her, as I promised. I am her True Knight. You heard me called that. Well I am doing my duty, My Lady Charlotina.'

'You are vague, Doctor Volospion.'

'Oh, madam, recall that encounter when we stood upon the cliff above Mr Bloom's ship!'

She drew her beautiful brows together. 'You acted uncharacteristically, as I remember.'

'You thought so.'

'Oh,' she was again impatient. 'Yes, yes . . .'

'Mr Bloom noticed, do you think?'

'He remarked on it, did he not?'

Doctor Volospion brought his hands together at his groin, his maroon and white sleeves swirling. He had an expression upon his pale, ascetic features of extreme self-satisfaction.

'Miss Ming,' he said, 'is safe in my castle. A force-field, quite as strong as the Fireclown's, surrounds it. For her own good, she cannot leave its confines.'

'You have locked her up?'

'For her own good. She agreed, for she fears the Fireclown greatly. I merely pointed out to her that it was the best way of ensuring that she would never encounter him.'

'In your menagerie?'

'She is comfortable, secure and, doubtless, happy,' said Doctor Volospion.

'True Knight, say you? Sorcerer, more accurately!' My Lady Charlotina for the first time showed admiration of Doctor Volospion's cunning. 'I see! Excellent!'

Doctor Volospion's thin smile was almost joyous. His cold eyes sparkled. 'I shall show you, I think, that I am no mere shadow of Jagged.'

'Did anyone suggest ...?'

'If anyone did suggest such a thing, they shall be proved in error.'

She pursed her lips and looked at first one of her feet and then the other. 'If the plan works ...'

'It will work. The art of conflict is to turn the antagonist's own strengths against him and to draw out his weaknesses.'

'It is one interpretation of the art. There have been so many, down all these millions of days.'

'You shall see, madam.'

'The Fireclown knows what you have done?'

'He has already accused me of it.'

'Well, you shall have the gratitude of each of us if you succeed, Doctor Volospion.'

'It is all I wish.'

The ground shook. They both turned, to see a magnificent pink pachyderm lumbering towards them. The beast bore a swaying howdah in which were seated both Abu Thaleb and Argonheart Po.

Abu Thaleb, in quilted silks of rose and sable, leaned down to greet them. 'My Lady Charlotina! I see music! And my old friend, Volospion. It has been so long ...'

'I will leave you to this reunion,' murmured My Lady Charlotina, and with a curtsy to the Commissar of Bengal she departed.

'Have you been all this time in your castle, Volospion?' asked Abu Thaleb. 'We have not met since that time when we were all three together, Argonheart, you and I, when Mr Bloom's ship had first landed. I have looked for you at many a gathering.'

'My attention, for my sins, has been much taken up with our current problem,' said Doctor Volospion.

'Ah, if only there were a solution,' rumbled Argonheart Po. 'We should have realised, when my dinosaurs were incinerated . . .'

'It was the moment to act, of course,' agreed Doctor Volospion. His neck grew stiff with craning and he lowered his head.

'It needs only Miss Ming,' said Abu Thaleb, lowering himself over the side of the howdah and beginning to descend by means of a golden rope-ladder the side of his great beast, 'to complete the original quartet.'

'She cannot be with us. She remains in safety in my castle.'

'Probably wise.' Abu Thaleb reached the ground. He signed for Argonheart Po that his way was now clear. The monstrous chef heaved his bulk gingerly to the edge and put a tentative foot upon a golden rung. Doctor Volospion watched with some fascination as the corpulent figure, swathed in white, came down the pink expanse.

'It is my duty to protect the lady from any danger,' Doctor Volospion said with a certain semblance of piety.

'She must be very much pleased by your thoughtfulness. She is so lacking in inner tranquillity that the trappings of security, physical and tactile, must mean much to her.'

'I think so.'

'Of course,' said Abu Thaleb doubtfully, 'this will confirm Mr Bloom's suspicions of you. Are you sure——?'

'I shall have to bear those suspicions, as a gentleman. I do my duty. If my actions are misinterpreted, particularly by Mr Bloom, that is no fault of mine.'

'Naturally.' Abu Thaleb dismissed his elephant. 'But if Mr Bloom were to take it into his head to—um—rescue Miss Ming?'

'I am prepared.'

Argonheart Po grunted. 'You are looking paler than ever, Doctor Volospion. You should eat more.'

'More? I do not eat at all.'

'There is more to eating than merely sustaining the flesh,' said Argonheart Po pointedly. 'If it comes to that, none of us *needs* to eat, there are so many quicker ways of absorbing energy, but there is a certain instinctive relish to such old-fashioned activities which it is as well to enjoy. After all, we are all human. Well, most of us.'

Abu Thaleb was upset by what seemed to him to be one friend's criticism of another. 'Argonheart, my dear, we all have preferences. Doctor Volospion enjoys rather more intellectual pastimes than do we. We must respect his tastes.'

Argonheart Po was quick to apologise. 'I did not mean to infer . . .'

'I detected no inference,' said Doctor Volospion with an extravagant wave of his hand. 'My interests, as you must know, are specialised. I study ancient faiths and have little time for anything else. It is perhaps because I would wish to believe in something supernatural. However, in all my studies I have yet to find something which cannot be explained or dismissed either as natural or as delusion. I do, admittedly, possess one or two miraculous artifacts which would *seem* to possess qualities not easily defined by science, but I fear it is only lack of knowledge on my part, and that these, too, will be shown to be the products of man's ingenuity.'

Argonheart Po smiled. 'If, one day, you will let me, I shall produce a culinary miracle for you and defy you to detect all the flavours and textures I shall put into it.'

'One day, perhaps, I should be honoured, mighty King of the Kitchen.'

And to Abu Thaleb's relief, the two parted amicably.

Doctor Volospion, alone for the moment, glanced about him. He seemed unusually content. A little sigh of pleasure passed between his normally tight-pressed lips. He could, upon occasions, produce in himself a semblance of gaiety and now there was a lightness to his step as he moved to greet Mistress Christia, the Everlasting Concubine, changing his costume as he went, to brilliant damson doublet and hose, curling shoes, a hat with a high crown and an elongated peak which could be doffed to brush the turf with a flourish as he bowed low. 'Beautiful Christia, Queen of my Heart, how I have longed for this opportunity to see you alone!'

Mistress Christia wore ringlets today of light red-gold, a translucent gown of sea green antique rayon, bracelets of live lizards, their tails held between their tiny forepaws.

'Oh, Doctor Volospion, how you flatter me! I have heard that you keep the most sought-after beauty in the world imprisoned in one of your gloomy towers!'

'You have heard? Already? It is true.' He pretended shame. 'I cannot help it. I am sworn to do so.'

'It is fitting, then, that you dally with me—for my reputation—'

'Is enviable,' he said.

She kissed his chilly cheek. 'But I know you to be heartless.'

'It is you, Mistress Christia, who gives me a heart.'

'But you will lay it at another's feet, I know. It is my fate, always.'

His attention was distracted, all at once. Sweet Orb Mace's juvenile slaughter-house was blazing. And a look of joy crossed Doctor Volospion's face.

Mistress Christia was bemused. 'You seem pleased at this? Poor Sweet Orb Mace and his lovely little house.'

'Oh, no, no, that is not it, at all.' He moved like a moth for the flames, his face lit by them. And then fire licked his body again and he was naked. There came a chorus from all around. Everyone was likewise unclad.

From out of the inferno stepped Emmanuel Bloom. He wore a black and white pierrot costume.

'I have come,' he trilled amiably, 'to be worshipped. I strip you naked. Thus I will strip your souls.' He looked at their

103

bare bodies and seemed rather confounded by some of the sights.

Fussing, a number of the guests were already replenishing themselves. Costumes blossomed on flesh again.

'No matter,' said the Fireclown, 'I have made my moral point.'

With a caress Doctor Volospion brought rippling velvet to his body, dark reds and greens glowed upon him. 'Shall you never tire of these demonstrations?' he asked.

Emmanuel Bloom shrugged. 'Why should I? It is my way of preaching to you. There are many excellent precedents for the method. A miracle and a parable or two work, as it were, wonders.'

'You have converted no one, sir,' said My Lady Charlotina, in a huge china bell, decorated with little flowers. Her voice tended to echo.

The Fireclown agreed with her. 'It is taking longer than I expected, madam. But I am persistent, by nature. And patient, in my way.'

'Well, sir, we lose patience,' said Abu Thaleb. 'I regret to say it, but it is true.' He turned for confirmation to his friends. All nodded. 'You see?'

'Is consensus truth?' the Fireclown wished to know. 'Agree what you like between yourselves, for it will not alter what is so.'

'It could be said that that which all are agreed upon is truth,' mildly proposed Argonheart Po, who saw the chance of a metaphysical spat. 'Do we not make the truth from the stuff of Chaos?'

'If the will is strong enough, perhaps,' said Emmanuel Bloom. 'But your wills are nothing. Mine is immeasurably powerful. You use gadgetry for your miracles. Do you see me using anything else but the power of my mind?'

'Your ship's force-field . . .' suggested Doctor Volospion.

'That, too, is controlled by my mind.'

Doctor Volospion seemed unhappy with this information.

'And where is my soulmate?' inquired Mr Bloom. 'Where is my consort? Where are you hiding her, Volospion? Eh, manikin? Speak!' He glared up at his smiling adversary.

'She is protected,' said Volospion, 'from you.'

'Protected? She needs no protection from Emmanuel Bloom. So, you imprison her.'

'For her own safety,' said My Lady Charlotina. 'It is what Miss Ming wants.'

'She is deluded.' The Fireclown displayed irritation. 'Deluded by this conjuror and his jesuitry. Give her up to me. I demand it. If I can save no other soul in this whole world, I shall save hers, I swear!'

'Never,' said Doctor Volospion, 'would I give another human creature into your keeping. How could I justify my conscience?'

'Conscience! Pah!'

'She is secure,' My Lady Charlotina glanced once at Doctor Volospion, 'is she not? Locked in your deepest dungeon?'

'Well ...' Doctor Volospion's shrug was modest.

'Ah, I cannot bear it! Know this, creeping jackal, sniggering quasi-priest, that I shall release her. I shall rescue her from any prison you may conceive. Why do you do this? Do you bargain with me?'

'Bargain?' said Doctor Volospion. 'What have you that I should wish to bargain?'

'What do you wish from me?' The Fireclown had become agitated. 'Tell me!'

'Nothing. You have heard my reasons for keeping Miss Ming safe from your threats ...'

'Threats? When did I threaten?'

'You have frightened the poor woman. She is not very intelligent. She has scant self-confidence ...'

'I offer her all of that and more. It is promises, not threats, I make! Bah!' The Fireclown set the lawn to smouldering and, as a consequence, many of the guests to dancing. At length everyone withdrew a few feet into the air, though still disturbed by rich smoke. Only the Fireclown remained on the ground, careless of the heat. 'I can give that woman everything. You take from her what little pride she still has. I can give her beauty and love and eternal life ...'

105

'The secret of eternal life, Mr Bloom, is already known to us,' said My Lady Charlotina from above. She had some difficulty in seeing him through the smoke, which grew steadily thicker.

'This? It is a state of eternal death. You have no true enthusiasms any longer. The secret of eternal life, madam, is enthusiasm, nothing more or less.'

'Enough?' said a distant Argonheart Po. 'To sustain us physically?'

'To relish everything to the full, for its own sake, that's the answer.' Mr Bloom's black and white pierrot costume was almost invisible now in the boiling smoke. 'Away with your charms and potions, your Shangri Las, your planets of Youth, of frozen cells and brain transfers!—many's the entity I've seen last little more than a thousand years before boredom shrivels up his soul and kills him.'

'Kills him?' Argonheart's voice was even fainter.

'Oh, his body may live. But one way or another, boredom kills him!'

'Your ideas remain somewhat out of date,' said My Lady Charlotina. 'Immortality is no longer a matter of potions, enchantments or surgery ...'

'I speak of the soul, madam.'

'Then you speak of nothing at all,' said Doctor Volospion.

There was no reply.

The Fireclown was gone.

CHAPTER ELEVEN

*In which Doctor Volospion is Subjected to a
Siege and Attempts to Parley*

Miss Ming was neither chained nor bound, neither did she languish in a dungeon, but she did confine herself, at Doctor Volospion's request, to her own apartments, furnished by him to her exact requirements, and at first she was content to accept this security. But as time passed she came to pine for human company, for even Doctor Volospion hardly ever visited her, and her only exchanges were with mechanical servants. When she did encounter her dark-minded host she would beg for news of Bloom, praying that by now he would have abandoned his plans and left the planet.

She saw Doctor Volospion soon after the party at Sweet Orb Mace's, where the house and lawn had been burned.

'He is still, I fear, here,' Volospion informed her, seating himself on a pink, quilted pouf. 'His determination to save the world has weakened just a little, I would say.'

'So he will go soon?'

'His determination to win your hand, Miss Ming, is if anything stronger than ever.'

'So he remains ...' She sank upon a satin cushion.

'Everyone shares your dismay. Indeed, I have been deputised to rid the world of the madman, in an informal way, and I have racked my brains to conceive a plan, but none comes. Can you think of anything?'

'Me? Little Mavis? I'm very honoured, Doctor Volospion, but ...' She played with the neck of her blue lace negligée. 'If you have failed, how can *I* help?'

'I thought you might have a better understanding of your

suitor's mentality. He loves you very much. He told me so again, at the party. He accused me of keeping you here against your will.'

She uttered her familiar tinkling laugh. 'Against my will? What does he intend to do, but carry me off!' She shuddered.

'Quite.'

'I still can't believe he was serious,' she said. 'Can you?'

'He is deeply serious. He is a man of much experience. That we know. He has considerable learning and his powers are impressive. As a lover, you could know worse, Miss Ming.'

'He's repulsive.'

Doctor Volospion rose from the pouf. 'As you say. Well— why, what is that beyond the window?'

The window to which he pointed was large but filled with small panels of thick glass, obscured, moreover, by the frothy blue curtains on either side of it, reminiscent of the ornament on a baby's cradle, the ribbons being pink and yellow.

It seemed that a small nova flared above the dour landscape of brooding trees and rocks surrounding Castle Volospion. The light approached them and then began to fall, just short of the force-field which protected the whole vast building (or series of buildings, as they actually were). Its colour changed from white to glowing red and it became identifiable as Emmanuel Bloom's baroque spacecraft.

'Oh, no!' wailed Miss Ming.

'Rest assured,' said Doctor Volospion. 'My force-field, like his own, is impregnable. He cannot enter.'

The vessel landed, destroying a tree or two as it did so and turning rocks to a pool of black glass.

Miss Ming fled hastily to the window and drew the curtains. 'There! This is torment, Doctor Volospion. I'm so unhappy!' She began to weep.

'I will do what I can,' he said, 'to dissuade him, but I can make no promises. He is so dedicated.'

'You'll go to see him?' She snuffled. Her blue eyes begged. 'You'll make him go away?'

'As I said—'

'Oh! Can't you kill him? Can't you?'

108

'Kill? What a waste that would be of such an authentic messiah . . .'

'You're still thinking of yourself. What about me?'

'Of course, I know that you are feeling some stress but, perhaps with your help, I could solve our problem.'

'You could?' She dried her eyes upon her lacey sleeve.

'It would demand from you, Miss Ming, considerable courage, but the end would, I assure you, be worthwhile to us all.'

'What?'

'I shall tell you if and when the opportunity arises.'

'Not now?'

'Not yet.'

'I'll do anything,' she said, 'to be rid of him.'

'Good,' he said. He left her apartments.

Doctor Volospion strode, in ornamental green and black, through the candle-light of his corridors, climbing stairs of grey–brown stone until he had reached a roof. Into the late evening air, which he favoured, he stepped, upon his battlements, to peruse the Fireclown's ship.

Doctor Volospion laughed and his joy was mysterious. 'So, sir, you lay siege to my castle!'

His voice echoed from many parts of his stronghold, from massive towers, from steeples and from eaves. A cool breeze blew at his robes as he stood there in his pride and his mockery. Behind him stretched bridges without function, buttresses which gave support to nothing, domes which sheltered only empty air. Above were dark masses of cloud in a sky the colour of steel. Below, lurid and out of key with all these surroundings, stood the spaceship.

'I warn you, sir, you shall be resisted!' continued Doctor Volospion.

But there was still no reply.

'Miss Ming is in my charge. I have sworn an oath to protect her!'

The airlock hatch swung back. Little tongues of flame came forth and dissipated in the dank air. The ramp licked out and touched the glassy rock and the Fireclown made his appearance. He wore a scarlet cap and a jerkin of red and yellow

109

stripes. One leg was amber and the other orange, one foot, with bell-toed shoes, matched the red of his jerkin and the other matched the yellow. He had painted his face so that it was now the ridiculous mask of a traditional clown of antiquity and yet, withall, Doctor Volospion received the impression that Emmanuel Bloom was dressed for battle. Doctor Volospion smiled.

The thin, bird-like voice rose to the battlements. 'Let the woman go free!'

'She fears you, sir,' said Doctor Volospion equably. 'She begs me to slay you.'

'Of course, of course. It is because, like so many mortals, she is terror-struck by some hint of what I can release in her. But that is of no consequence, at this moment. You must remove yourself from the position you have taken between us.'

Emmanuel Bloom walked in poorly coordinated strides down his ramp, crossed the grass and was halted by the force-field. 'Remove this,' he commanded.

'I cannot,' Doctor Volospion told him.

'You must!'

'My pledge to Miss Ming ...'

'Is meaningless, as well you know. You serve only yourself. It is your doom ever to serve yourself and thus never to know true life!'

'You invent a role for me as you invent one for Miss Ming. Even your own role is invented. Your imagination, sir, is disordered. I advise you, with all courtesy, to leave, or change your ways, or alter your ambitions. This masquerade of yours will bring you only misery.' Doctor Volospion adopted the voice of sympathy.

'Must I suffer further examples of your hypocrisy, manikin? Let down this screen and show me to my soulmate.' Emmanuel Bloom banged a small fist upon the field, causing it to shimmer somewhat. His mad blue eyes were fierce and paradoxical in their setting of paint.

'Your "soulmate" sir, reviles you.'

'Your interpretations are of no interest to me. Let me see her!'

110

'If you saw her, she would confirm my words.'

'Her voice, perhaps, but not her soul.'

'I'll indulge you no further, sir.' Doctor Volospion turned from the battlements.

Behind him there came a most terrible tumult. He felt heat upon his back. He whirled. The Fireclown could not be seen, for now a wall of flame reared in place of the force-field. And the wall screamed.

Doctor Volospion touched a power ring and the flames became transparent ice through which he could just make out the silhouette of the Fireclown.

'Mr Bloom!' he called. 'We can play thus for many a century and consume all our energies. If I admitted you, would you give me your word that you would use no violence against either myself or Miss Ming, that you would not attempt to achieve your ends with force?'

'I never use force. I use my power to produce living parables, that is all, and so convince those who would oppose me.'

'But you would give your word?'

'If you require it, you have it.' And then the Fireclown raised his shadowy fist again and struck at the ice which shattered. He strode through the hole he had made. 'But you see how easily I can dispose of your protection!'

Doctor Volospion hid his mouth behind his hand. 'Ah, I had not realised ...' He lowered his lids so that his eyes might not be seen, yet it might have been that a cunning humour glittered there for a moment.

'Will you admit me to your castle, Doctor Volospion, so that I may see Miss Ming for myself?'

'Give me a little while so that I may prepare the lady for your visit. You will dine with me?'

'I will undergo any ritual you wish, but when I leave, it shall be with Mavis Ming, my love.'

'You gave your word ...'

'I gave my word and I shall keep it.'

Doctor Volospion quit his battlements.

CHAPTER TWELVE

In which Doctor Volospion Gives a Tour of his
Museum and his Menagerie of
Forgotten Faiths

Mavis Ming was desolate.

'Oh, you have betrayed me!'

'Betrayed?' Doctor Volospion laid a hand upon her trembling shoulder. 'Nothing of the sort. This is all part of my plan. I beg you to become an actress, Miss Ming. Show, as best you can, some little sympathy for your suitor. It will benefit you in the end.'

'You're laying a trap for him, aren't you?'

'I can only say, now, that you will soon be free of him.'

'You're certain.'

'Certain.'

'I'm not sure I could keep it up.'

'Trust me. I have so far proved myself your loyal protector, have I not?'

'Of course. I didn't mean to imply ...' She was hasty to give him reassurance.

'Then dress yourself and join us, as soon as you can, for dinner.'

'You'll be eating? You never—'

'It is the ceremony which is important.'

She nodded. 'All right.'

He crossed to the door. She said: 'He's not really very intelligent, is he?'

'I think not.'

'And you're very clever indeed.'

'You are kind.'

'What I mean is, I'm sure you *can* trick him, Doctor Volospion, if that's what you mean to do.'

'I appreciate your encouragement, Miss Ming.' He went out.

Mavis looked to her wardrobe. She dragged from it an evening dress of green and purple silk. She passed to her mirror and looked with displeasure upon her red-rimmed eyes, her bedraggled hair. 'Chin up, Mavis,' she said, 'it'll all be over soon. And it means you can go visiting again. What a relief that'll be! And if I play my part right, they'll have me to thank, as well as Doctor Volospion. I'll get a bit of respect.' She settled to her toilet.

It was to her credit that she made the most of herself, in her own eyes. She curled her hair so that it hung in blonde waves upon her shoulders. She applied plenty of mascara, to make her eyes look larger. She was relatively subtle with her rouge and she touched her best perfumed deodorant to all those parts of her body which, in her opinion, might require it (her cosmetics were largely twentieth century, created for her by Doctor Volospion at her request, for she considered the cosmetics of her own time to be crude and synthetic by comparison). She arranged an everlasting orchid upon her dress; she donned diamond earrings, a matching necklace, bracelets. 'Good enough to dine with the Emperor of Africa,' she said of herself, when she was ready.

She left her apartments and began her journey through passages which, in her opinion, Doctor Volospion kept unnecessarily dark, although, as she knew, it was done for the artistic effect he favoured.

At last she reached the great, gloomy hall where Doctor Volospion normally entertained his guests. Hard-faced metal servants already waited on the long table at one end of which sat dignified Doctor Volospion, and the pipsqueak Bloom, dressed in the silliest outfit Mavis Ming had ever seen. Strips of ancient neon, blue-white, illuminated this particular part of the castle, though they had been designed to malfunction and so flickered on and off, creating sudden shadows and brilliances which always disturbed Miss Ming. The walls

113

were of undressed stone and bore no decoration save the tall portrait of Doctor Volospion over the massive fireplace in which a small electric fire had been positioned, the fire was also an antique, designed to simulate burning coal.

Becoming aware of her entrance, both men rose from their seats.

'My madonna!' breathed Bloom.

'Good evening, Miss Ming.' Doctor Volospion bowed.

Emmanuel Bloom seemed to be making an effort to contain himself. He sat down again.

'Good evening, gentlemen.' She responded to this effort with one of her own. 'How nice to see you again, Mr Bloom!'

'Oh!' He lifted a chop to his grease-painted mouth.

Simple food was placed by servants before her. She sat at Doctor Volospion's left. She had no appetite, but she made some show of eating, noting that Doctor Volospion did the same. She hoped that Bloom would not subject them to any more of his megalomaniacal monologues. It was still difficult to understand why a man of Doctor Volospion's intelligence indulged Bloom at all, and yet they seemed to converse readily enough.

'You deal, sir, in Ideals,' Doctor Volospion was saying, 'I, in Realities: though I remain fascinated by the trappings by means of which men seek to give credence to their dreamings.'

'The trappings are all you can ever know,' said the Fireclown, 'for you can never experience the ecstasy of Faith. You are too empty.'

'You continue to be hard on me, sir, while I try—'

'I speak the truth.'

'Ah, well. I suppose you do read me aright, Mr Bloom.'

'Of course, I do. I gave my word only that I should not take Miss Ming from here by force. I did not agree to join in your courtesies, your hypocrisies. What are your manners when seen in the light of the great unchangeable realities of the Multiverse?'

'Your belief in the permanence of anything, Mr Bloom, is incredible to me. Everything is transitory. Can the experience of a billion years have taught you nothing?'

114

'On the contrary, Doctor Volospion.' He did not amplify. He chewed at his chop.

'Has experience left you untouched? Were you ever the same?'

'I suppose my character has changed little. I have known the punishments of Prometheus, but I have been that god's persecutor, too—for Bloom has bloomed everywhere, in every guise . . .'

'More peas?' interrupted Miss Ming.

Emmanuel Bloom shook his head.

'But creed has followed creed, movement followed movement, down all the centuries,' continued Doctor Volospion, 'and not one important change in any of them, though millions have lost their lives over some slight interpretation. Are men not fools to destroy themselves thus? Questing after impossibilities, golden dreams, romantic fancies, perfection . . .'

'Oh, certainly. Clowns, all of them. Like me.'

Doctor Volospion did not know what to make of this.

'You agree?'

'The clown weeps, laughs, knows joy and sorrow. It is not enough to look at his costume and laugh and say—here is mankind revealed. Irony is nothing by itself. Irony is a modifier, not a protection. We live our lives because we have only our lives to live.'

'Um,' said Doctor Volospion. 'I think I should show you my collection. I possess mementoes of a million creeds.' He pointed with his thumb at the floor. 'Down there.'

'I doubt that they will be unfamiliar to me,' said Bloom. 'What do you hope to prove?'

'That you are not original, I suppose.'

'And by this means you think you will encourage me to leave your planet without a single pledge fulfilled?'

Doctor Volospion made a gesture. 'You read me so well, Mr Bloom.'

'I'll inspect this stuff, if you wish. I am curious. I am respectful, too, of all prophets and all objects of devotion, but as to my originality . . .'

'Well,' said Doctor Volospion, 'we shall see. If you will

115

allow me to conduct you upon a brief tour of my collection, I shall hope to convince you.'

'Miss Ming will accompany us?'

'Oh, I'd love to,' said Miss Ming courageously. She hated Doctor Volospion's treasures.

'I think my collection is the greatest in the Universe,' continued Doctor Volospion. 'No better has existed, certainly, in Earth's history. Many missionaries have come this way. Most have made attempts to—um—save us. As you have. They have not been, in the main, as spectacular, I will admit, nor have they claimed as much as you claim. However ...' He took a pea upon his fork. There was something in the gesture to make Mavis Ming suspect that he planned something more than a mere tour of his treasures. '... you would agree that your arguments are scarcely subtle. They allow for no nuance.'

Now nothing would stop the Fireclown. He rose from the table, his birdlike movements even more exaggerated than usual. He strutted the length of the table. He strutted back again. 'A pox on nuance! Seize the substance, beak and claws, and leave the chitterlings for the carrion! Let crows and storks squabble over the scraps, these subtleties—the eagle takes the main carcass, as much or as little as he needs!' He fixed his gaze upon Miss Ming. 'Forget your quibbling scruples, madonna! Come with me now. Together we'll leave the planet to its fate. Their souls gutter like dying candles. The whole world reeks of inertia. If they will not have my Ideals, then I shall bestow *all* my gifts on you!'

Mavis Ming said in strangled tones: 'You are very kind, Mr Bloom, but ...'

'Perhaps that particular matter can be discussed later,' proposed Doctor Volospion tightening his cap about his head and face. 'Now, sir, if you will come?'

'Miss Ming, too?'

'Miss Ming.'

The trio left the hall, with Miss Ming reluctantly trailing behind. She desperately hoped that Doctor Volospion was not playing one of his games at her expense. He had been so nice to her lately, she thought, that he was evidently mellowing her, yet she hated in herself that slight lingering suspicion of him, that voice which had told her, on more than one occasion, that if someone liked her, then that someone could have no taste at all and was therefore not worth knowing.

They descended and they descended, for it was Doctor Volospion's pleasure to bury his collection in the bowels of his castle. Murky corridor followed murky corridor, lit by flambeaux, candles, rush torches, oil-lamps, anything that would give the minimum of light and cast the maximum number of shadows.

'You have,' said Mr Bloom after some while of this tramping, 'an unexceptional imagination, Doctor Volospion.'

'I do not concern myself with the lust for variation enjoyed by most of my fellows at the End of Time,' remarked the lean man. 'I follow but a few simple obsessions. And in that, I think, we share something, Mr Bloom.'

'Well—' began the Fireclown.

But then Doctor Volospion had stopped at an ironbound door. 'Here we are!' He flung the door wide. The light from within seemed intense.

The Fireclown strutted, stiff-limbed as ever, into the high vaulted hall. He blinked in the light. He sniffed the warm, heavy air. For almost as far as the eye could see there were rows and rows of cabinets, pedestals, display domes; Doctor Volospion's museum.

'What's this?' inquired Mr Bloom.

'My collection of devotional objects, culled from all Ages. From all the planets of the Universe.' Doctor Volospion was proud.

It was difficult to see if Mr Bloom was impressed, for his clown's paint hid most expression.

Doctor Volospion paused beside a little table. 'Only the best have been preserved. I have discarded or destroyed the rest. Here is a history of folly!' He looked down at the table. On it lay a dusty scrap of skin to which clung a few faded feathers. Doctor Volospion plucked it up. 'Do you recognise that, Mr Bloom, with all your experience of Time and Space?'

The long neck came forwards to inspect the thing. 'The

remains of a fowl?' suggested Mr Bloom. 'A chicken, perhaps?'

Miss Ming wrinkled her nose and backed away from them. 'I never liked this part of the castle. It's creepy. I don't know how—' She pulled herself together.

'Eh?' said Mr Bloom.

Doctor Volospion permitted a dark smile. 'It is all that remains of Yawk, Saviour of Shakah, founder of a religion which spread through fourteen star-systems and eighty planets and lasted some seven thousand years until it became the subject of a jehad.'

'Hm,' said Mr Bloom non-committally.

'I had this,' confided Doctor Volospion, 'from the last living being to retain his faith in Yawk. He regarded himself as the only guardian of the relic, carried it across countless light-years, preaching the gospel of Yawk (and a fine, poetic tale it is), until he reached Earth.'

'And then?' Bloom reverently replaced the piece of skin.

'He is now a guest of mine. You will meet him later.'

A smile appeared momentarily on Miss Ming's lips. She believed that she had guessed what her host had in mind.

'Aha,' murmured the Fireclown. 'And what would this be?' He moved on through the hall, pausing beside a cabinet containing an oddly wrought artifact made of something resembling green marble.

'A weapon,' said Volospion. 'The very gun which slew Marchbanks, the Martyr of Mars, during the revival, in the twenty-fifth century (A.D., of course), of the famous Kangaroo Cult which had swept the solar system about a hundred years previously, before it was superseded by some atheistic political doctrine. You know how one is prone to follow the other. Nothing, Mr Bloom, changes very much, either in the fundamentals or the rhetoric of religions and political creeds. I hope I am not depressing you?'

Bloom snorted. 'How could you? None of these others has experienced what I have experienced. None has had the knowledge I have gained and, admittedly, half-forgotten. Do not confuse me with these, I warn you, Doctor Volospion, if you wish to continue to converse with me. I could destroy all this in a moment, if I wished, and it would make no difference ...'

'You threaten?'

'What?' The little man removed his clown's cap and ran his fingers through the tangles of his auburn hair. 'Eh? Threaten? Don't be foolish. I gave my word. I was merely lending emphasis to my statement.'

'Besides,' said Doctor Volospion smoothly. 'You could do little now, I suspect, for there are several force-fields lying between you and your ship now—they protect my museum —and I suspect that your ship is the main source of your power, for all you claim it derives entirely from your mind.'

Emmanuel Bloom chuckled. 'You have found me out, Doctor Volospion, I see.' He seemed undisturbed. 'Now, then, what other pathetic monuments to the nobility of the human spirit have you locked up here?'

Doctor Volospion extended his arms. 'What would you see?' He pointed in one direction. 'A wheel from Krishna's chariot?' He pointed in another. 'A tooth said to belong to the Buddha? One of the original Tablets of Moses? Bunter's bottle? The sacred crown of the Kennedys? Hitler's nail? There,' he tapped a dome, 'you'll find them all in that case. Or over here,' a sweep of a green and black arm, 'the finger-bones of Karl Marx, the knee-cap of Mao Tse-tung, a mummified testicle belonging to Heffner, the skeleton of Maluk Khan, the tongue of Suhulu. Or what of these? Filp's loin-cloth, Xiombarg's napkin, Teglardin's peach rag. Then there are the coins of Bibb-Nardrop, the silver wands of Er and Er, the towels of Ich—all the way from a world within the Crab Nebula. And most of these, in this section here, are only from the Dawn Age. Farther along are relics from all other Ages of this world and the Universe. Rags and bones, Mr Bloom. Rags and bones.'

'I am moved,' said Emmanuel Bloom.

'All that is left,' said Doctor Volospion, 'of a million mighty causes. And all, at core, that those causes ever were!'

The clown's face was grave as he moved among the cases.

119

Mavis Ming was shivering. 'This place really *does* depress me,' she whispered to her guardian. 'I know it's my fault, but I've always hated places like this. They seem ghoulish. Not that I'm criticising, Doctor Volospion, but I've never been able to understand why a man like you could indulge in such a strange hobby. It's all research material, of course. We have to do research, don't we? Well, at least, you do. It's nice that someone does. I mean this is your area of research, isn't it, this particular aspect of the galaxy's past? It's why I'll never make a first-rank historian, I suppose. It's the same, you know, when I lived with Donny Stevens. It was the cold-blooded killing of those sweet little rabbits and monkeys at the lab. I simply refused, you know, to let him or anyone else talk about it when I was around. And with the time machine, too, they sent so many to God knows where before they'd got it working properly. When can I stop this charade, Doctor ...?'

Volospion raised a finger to his lips. Bloom was some distance away but had turned, detecting the voice, no doubt, of his loved one.

'Rags and bones,' said Doctor Volospion, as if he had been reiterating his opinions to Miss Ming.

'No,' called Bloom from where he stood beside a case containing many slightly differently shaped strips of metal, 'these were merely the instruments used to focus faith. Witness their variety. Anything would do as a lense to harness the soul's fire. A bit of wood. A stone. A cup. A custard pie. Nothing here means anything without the presence of the beings who believed in their validity. Whether that piece of worm-eaten wood really did come from Christ's cross or not is immaterial. As a symbol ...'

'You question the authenticity of my prizes?'

'It is not important ...'

Doctor Volospion betrayed agitation. It was genuine. 'It is to me, Mr Bloom. I will have nothing in my museum that is not authentic!'

'So you have a faith of your own, after all.' Bloom's painted lips formed a smile.

He leaned, a tiny jester, a cockerel, against a force dome.

Doctor Volospion lost none of his composure. 'If you mean that I pride myself on my ability to sniff out any fakes, any piece of doubtful origin, then you speak rightly. I have faith in my own taste and judgement. But come, let us move on. It is not the museum that I wish you to inspect, but the menagerie, which is of greater interest, for there ...'

'Show me this cup you have. This Holy Grail. I was looking for it.'

'Well, if you feel you have the leisure. Certainly. There it is. In the cabinet with Jissard's space-helmet and Panjit's belt.'

Emmanuel Bloom trotted rapidly in the direction indicated by Doctor Volospion, weaving his way among the various displays, until he came to the far wall where, behind a slightly quivering energy screen, between the helmet and the belt, stood a pulsing, golden cup, semi-transparent, in which a red liquid swirled.

Bloom's glance at the cup was casual. He made no serious attempt to inspect it. He turned back to Doctor Volospion, who had followed behind.

'Well?' said Volospion.

Bloom laughed. 'Your taste and judgement fail you, Doctor Volospion. It is a fake, that Grail.'

'How could you know?'

'I assure you that I am right.'

Bloom began to leave the case, but Doctor Volospion tugged at his arm. 'You would argue that it is merely mythical, wouldn't you? That it never existed. Yet there is proof that it did.'

'Oh, I need no proof of the Grail's existence. But if it were the true Grail how could you, of all people, keep it?'

Doctor Volospion frowned. 'You are vaguer than usual, Mr Bloom. I keep the cup because it is mine.'

'Yours?'

'I had it from a time traveller who had spent his entire life searching for it and who, as it happens, found it in one of our own cities. Unfortunately, the traveller destroyed himself soon after coming to stay with me. They are all mad, such people. But the thing itself is authentic. He had found many

121

fakes before he found the true Grail. He vouched for this one. And he should have known, a man who had dedicated himself to his quest and who was willing to kill himself once that quest was over.'

'He probably thought it would bring him back to life,' mused the Fireclown. 'That is part of the legend, you know. One of the real Grail's minor properties.'

'Real? This man's opinion was irrefutable.'

'Well, I am glad that he is dead,' said Bloom, and then he laughed a strange, deep-throated laugh which had no business coming from that puny frame, 'for I should not have liked to have disappointed him.'

'Disappointed?' Volospion flushed. 'Now—'

'That cup is not even a very good copy of the original, Doctor Volospion.'

Doctor Volospion drew himself up and arranged the folds of his robe carefully in front of him. His voice was calm when he next spoke. 'How would you know such a thing, Mr Bloom? You claim great knowledge, yet you exhibit no signs of it in your rather foolish behaviour, your pointless pursuits. You dress a fool and you are a fool, say I.'

'Possibly. None the less, that Grail is a fake.'

'Why do you know?' Doctor Volospion's gaze was not quite as steady as it might have been.

'Because,' explained Bloom amicably, 'I am, among many other things, the Guardian of the Grail. That is to say, specifically, that I am graced by the presence of the Holy Grail.'

'What!' Doctor Volospion was openly contemptuous.

'You probably do not know,' Mr Bloom went on, 'that only those who are absolutely pure in spirit, who never commit the sin of accidia (moral torpor, if you prefer) may ever see the Grail and only one such as myself may ever receive the sacred trust of Joseph of Arimathaea, the Good Soldier, who carried the Grail to Glastonbury. I have had this trust for several centuries, at least. I am probably the only mortal being left alive who deserves the honour (though, of course, I am not so proud as to be certain of it). My ship is full of such things —relics to rival any of these here—collected in an eternity of wandering the many dimensions of the Universe, tumbling through Time, companion to chronons ...'

Doctor Volospion's face wore an expression quite different to anything Miss Ming had ever seen. He was deeply serious. His voice contained an unusual vibrancy.

'Oh, don't be taken in by him, Doctor Volospion,' she said, giving up any idea of trying to placate the Fireclown. 'He's an obvious charlatan.'

Bloom bowed. Doctor Volospion did not even hear her.

'How can you prove that your Grail is the original, Mr Bloom?'

'I do not have to *prove* such a thing. The Grail chooses its own guardian. The Grail will only appear to one whose Faith is Absolute. My Faith is Absolute.'

Bloom began to stride towards Mavis Ming. Volospion followed thoughtfully in his wake.

'Oo!' squeaked Miss Ming, seeing her protector distracted and fearing a sudden leap. 'Get off!'

'I am not, Miss Ming, on. I promise you no violence, not yet, not until you come to me.'

'Oh! You think that I'd—?' She struggled with her own revulsion and the remembrance of her promise to Doctor Volospion.

'You still make a pretence at resistance, I see.' Bloom beamed. 'Such is female pride. I came here to claim a world and now I willingly renounce that claim if it means that I can possess you, woman, body and soul. You are the most beautiful creature I have ever seen in all the aeons of my wandering. Mavis! Mavis! Music floods my being at the murmur of your exquisite name. Queen Mavis—Maeve, Sorceress Queen, Destroyer of Cuchulain, Beloved of the Sun— ah, you have the power to do it—but you shall not destroy me again, Beautiful Maeve. You shall find me in Fire and in Fire shall we be united!'

It was true that, for the first time, Miss Ming's expression began to soften, but Doctor Volospion came to her aid.

'I am sure Miss Ming is duly flattered,' he said. It was evident, with his next statement, that he merely resented the interruption to his line of thought. 'But as for the Holy Grail, you do not, I suppose, have it about you?'

'Of course not. It appears only at my prayer.'

'You can summon it to you?'

'No. It appears. During my meditations.'

'You would not care to meditate now? To prove that yours is the true one.'

'I have no urge to meditate.' Mr Bloom dismissed the Doctor from his attention and, hands outstretched in that stiff, awkward way of his, moved to embrace Miss Ming, only to pause as he felt Volospion's touch on his arm.

'It is in your ship, then?'

'It visits my ship, yes.'

'Visits?'

'Doctor Volospion. I have tried to explain to you clearly enough. The Grail you have is not a mystical artifact, no matter how miraculous it seems to be. The true Holy Grail *is* a mystical artifact and therefore it comes and goes, according to the spiritual ambience. That is why your so-called Grail is plainly a fake. If it were real, it would not be here!'

'This is mere obfuscation . . .'

'Doctor Volospion, you are a most obtuse creature.'

Miss Ming began to move slowly backwards.

'Mr Bloom, I ask only for illumination . . .'

'I try to bring it. But I have failed with you, as I have failed with everyone but Miss Ming. That is only to be expected of one who is not really alive at all. Can one hold an intelligent conversation with a corpse?'

'You are crudely insulting, Mr Bloom. There is no call . . .' Doctor Volospion had lost most of his usual self-control.

Mavis Ming, terrified of further conflict in which, somehow she knew she would be the worst sufferer, if her experience were anything to go by, broke in with a nervous yelp:

'Show Mr Bloom your menagerie, Doctor Volospion! The menagerie! The menagerie!'

Doctor Volospion turned glazed and dreaming eyes upon her. 'What?'

'The menagerie. There are many entities there that Mr

Bloom might wish to converse with.'

The Fireclown bent to straighten one of his long shoes and Mavis Ming seized the chance to wink broadly at Doctor Volospion.

'Ah, yes, the menagerie. Mr Bloom?'

'You wish to show me the menagerie?'

'Yes.'

'Then lead me to it,' said Bloom generously.

Doctor Volospion continued to brood as he advanced before them, through another series of gloomy passages whose gently sloping floors took them still deeper underground. Doctor Volospion had a tendency to favour the subterranean in almost everything.

By the time, however, that they had reached the series of chambers Doctor Volospion chose to call his 'crypts', their guide had resumed his normal manner of poised irony.

These halls were far larger than the museum. On either side were reproduced many different environments, in the manner of zoological gardens, in which were incarcerated his collection of creatures culled from countless cultures, some indigenous and others alien to Earth.

Enthusiasm returned to Volospion's voice as he pointed out his prizes while they progressed slowly down the central aisle.

'My Christians and my Hare Krishnans,' declaimed the doctor, 'my Moslems and my Marxists, my Jews and my Joy-pushers, my Dervishes, Buddhists, Hindus, Nature-worshippers, Confucians, Leavisites, Sufis, Shintoists, New Shintoists, Reformed Shintoists, Shinto-Scientologists, Mansonite Watersharers, Anthroposophists, Flumers, Haythornthwaitists, Fundamentalist Ouspenskyians, Sperm Worshippers, followers of the Five Larger Moon Devils, followers of the Stone that Cannot we Weighed, followers of the Sword and the Stallion, Awaiters of the Epoch, Mensans, Doo-en Skin Slicers, Crabbellied Milestriders, Poobem Wrigglers, Tribunites, Callagraphic Diviners, Betelgeusian Grass Sniffers, Aldebarran Grass Sniffers, Terran Grass Sniffers and Frexian Anti-Grass Sniffers. There are the Racists (Various)—I mix them together in the one environment because it makes for greater interest. The River of Blood was my own idea. It blends very well, I think, into the general landscape.' Doctor Volospion was evidently extremely proud of his collection. 'They are all, of course, in their normal environments. Every care is taken to see that they are preserved in the best of health and happiness. You will note, Mr Bloom, that the majority are content, so long as they are allowed to speak or perform the occasional small miracle.'

The Fireclown's attention seemed elsewhere.

'The sound,' said Doctor Volospion, and he touched a power ring, whereupon the air was filled with a babble of voices as prophets prophesied, preachers preached, messiahs announced various millenia, saviours summoned disciples, archbishops proclaimed Armageddon, fakirs mourned materialism, priests prayed, imans intoned, rabbis railed and druids droned. 'Enough?'

The Fireclown raised a hand in assent and Doctor Volospion touched the ring again so that much of the noise died away.

'Well, Mr Bloom, do you find these pronouncements essentially distinguishable from your own?'

But the Fireclown was again studying Mavis Ming who was, in turn, looking extremely self-conscious. She was blushing through her rouge. She pretended to take an interest in the sermon being delivered by a snail-like being from some remote world near the galaxy's centre.

'What?'

Bloom cocked an ear in Volospion's direction. 'Distinguishable? Oh, of course. Of course. I respect all the views being expressed. They are, I would agree, a little familiar, some of them. But these poor creatures lack either my power or my experience. I would guess, too, that they lack my courage. Or my purity of purpose. Why do you keep them locked up here?'

Doctor Volospion ignored the final sentence. 'Many would differ with you, I think.'

'Quite so. But you cease to entertain me, Doctor Volospion.

I have decided to take Miss Ming, my madonna, back to my ship now. The visit has been fairly interesting. More interesting than I believed it would be. Are you coming, Miss Ming?'

Miss Ming hesitated. She glanced at Doctor Volospion. 'Well, I—'

'Do not consult this corpse,' Mr Bloom told her. 'I shall be your mentor. It is my duty and destiny to remove you from this environment at once, to bring you to the knowledge of your own divinity!'

Mavis Ming breathed heavily, still flushed. Her eyes darted from Bloom to Volospion. 'I don't think you'll be removing either me *or* yourself from this castle, Mr Bloom.' She smiled openly now at Doctor Volospion and her eyes were full of hope and terror. They asked a hundred questions. She seemed close to panic and was poised to flee.

Emmanuel Bloom gave a snort of impatience. 'Miss Ming, my love, you are mine.' His high, fluting voice continued to trill, but it was plain that she no longer heard his words. His bird-like hands touched hers. She screamed.

'Doctor Volospion!'

Doctor Volospion was fully himself. 'It is hardly gentlemanly, as I have pointed out, to force your attentions upon a lady, Mr Bloom. I would remind you of your word.'

'I keep it. I use no violence.'

Doctor Volospion now appeared to be relishing the drama. The fingers of his left hand hovered over the fingers of his right, on which were most of his power rings.

The Fireclown's hands remained on Miss Ming's. 'He's really strong!' she cried. 'I can't get free, Doctor Volospion. Oo ...' It seemed that an almost euphoric weakness suffused her body now. She was panting, incapable of thought; her lips were dry, her tongue was dry, and the only word she could form was a whispered 'No'.

Doctor Volospion seemed ignorant of the degree of tension in the menagerie. Many of the prophets, both human and alien, had stopped their monologues and now pressed forward to watch the struggle.

Doctor Volospion said firmly: 'Mr Bloom, since you remain here as my guest, I would ask you to recall . . .'

The blue eyes became shrewd even as they stared into Mavis Ming's. 'Your guest? No longer. We leave. Do you come, Mavis mine?'

'I—I—' It was as if she wished to say yes to him, yet she continued to pull back as best she could.

'Mr Bloom, you have had your opportunity to leave this planet. You refused to take it. Well, now you have no choice. You shall stay for ever (which is not, we think, that long).'

Mr Bloom raised a knowing head. 'What?'

'You have told us, yourself, that you are unique, sir.' Doctor Volospion was triumphant. 'You prize yourself so highly, I must accept your valuation.'

'Eh?'

'From henceforth, Sir Prophet, you will grace my menagerie. Here you will stay—my finest acquisition.'

'What? My power!' Did Mr Bloom show genuine surprise? His gestures became melodramatic to a degree.

Doctor Volospion was too full of victory to detect play-acting, if play-acting there was. 'Here you may preach to your heart's content. You will find the competition stimulating, I am certain.'

Bloom received this intelligence calmly. 'My power is greater than yours,' he said.

'I led you to think that it was, so that you would feel confident when I suggested a tour of my collection. Twelve force-screens of unimaginable strength now lie between you and your ship, cutting you off from the source of your energy. Do you think you could have shattered my first force-field if I had not allowed it?'

'It seemed singularly easy,' agreed the Fireclown. 'But you seem still unclear as to the nature of my own power. It does not derive from a physical source, as yours does, though you are right in assuming it comes from my ship. It is spiritual inspiration which allows me to work my miracles. The source of that inspiration lies in the ship.'

'This so-called Grail of yours?'

Bloom fell silent.

128

'Well, call on it, then,' said Doctor Volospion.

Every scrap of bombast had disappeared from Bloom. It was as if he discarded a useless weapon, or rather a piece of armour which had proved defective. 'There is no entity more free in all the teeming Multiverse than the Fireclown.' His unblinking eyes stared into Miss Ming's again. 'You cannot imprison me, sir.'

'Imprison?' Doctor Volospion derided the idea with a gesture. 'You shall have everything you desire. Your favourite environment shall be recreated for you. If necessary, it is possible to supply the impression of distance, movement. Regard the state as well-earned retirement, Mr Bloom.'

The avian head turned on the long neck, the paint around the mouth formed an expression of some gravity (albeit exaggerated). Mr Bloom did not relax his grip upon Miss Ming's hands.

'Your satire palls, Doctor Volospion. It is the sort that easily grows stale, for it lacks love; it is inspired by self-hatred. You are typical of those faithless priests of the fifth millenium who were once your comrades in vice.'

Doctor Volospion showed shock. 'How could you possibly know my origins? The secret . . .'

'There are no secrets from the Sun,' said the Fireclown. 'The Sun knows All. Old He may be, but His memory is clearer than those of your poor, senescent cities.'

'Do not seek to confound me, sir, with airy generalities of that sort. How do you know?'

'I have eyes,' said Bloom, 'which have seen all things. One gesture reveals a society to me—two words reveal an individual. A conversation betrays every origin.'

'This Grail of yours? It helps you?'

The Fireclown ignored him. 'The eagle floats on currents of light, high above the world, and the light is recollection, the light is history. I know you, Doctor Volospion, and I know you for a villain, just as I know Mavis Ming as a goddess—chained and gagged, perverted and alone, but still a goddess.'

Doctor Volospion's laugh was cruel. 'All you do, Mr Bloom, is to reveal yourself as a buffoon! Not even your insane Faith can make an angel of Miss Ming!'

Mavis Ming was not resentful. 'I've got my good points,' she said, 'but I'm no Gloria Gutzmann. And I try too hard, I guess, and people don't like that. I can be neurotic, probably. After all, that affair with Snuffles didn't do anyone any good in the end though I was trying to do Dafnish Armatuce a favour.'

She babbled on, scarcely conscious of her words, while the adversaries, pausing in their conflict, watched her.

'But then, maybe I *was* acting selfishly, after all. Well, it's all water under the bridge, isn't it? What's done is done. Who can blame anybody, at the end of the day?'

Mr Bloom's voice became a caressing murmur. He stroked her hands. 'Fear not, Miss Ming. I am the Flame of Life. I carry a torch that will resurrect the spirit, and I carry a scourge to drive out devils. I need no armour, save my faith, my knowledge, my understanding. I am the Sun's soldier, keeper of His mysteries. Give yourself to me and become fully yourself, alive and free.'

Mavis Ming began to cry. The Fireclown's vivid mask smiled in a grotesque of sympathy.

'Come with me now,' said Bloom.

'I would remind you that you are powerless to leave,' said Doctor Volospion.

The Fireclown dropped her hands and turned so that his back was to her. His little frame twitched and trembled, his red-gold mass of hair might have been the bristling crest of some exotic fowl, his little hands clenched and unclenched at his sides, like claws, as his beautiful, musical voice filled that dreadful menagerie.

'Ah, Volospion, I should destroy you—but one cannot destroy the dead!'

Doctor Volospion was apparently unmoved. 'Possibly, Mr Bloom, but the dead can imprison the living, can they not? If that is so, I possess the advantage which men like myself have always possessed over men such as you.'

The Fireclown wheeled to grasp Miss Ming. She cried out: 'Stop him, Doctor Volospion, for Christ's sake!'

And at last Doctor Volospion's long hand touched a power ring and the Fireclown was surrounded by bars of blue, pulsing energy.

'Ha!' The clown capered this way and that, trying to free himself and then, as if reconciled, sat down on the floor, crossing his little legs, his blue eyes blinking up at them as if in sudden bewilderment.

Doctor Volospion smiled.

'Eagle, is it? Phoenix? I must admit that I see only a caged sparrow.'

Emmanuel Bloom paid him no heed. He addressed Mavis Ming.

'Free me,' he said. 'It will mean your own freedom.'

Mavis Ming giggled.

CHAPTER THIRTEEN

*In which Doctor Volospion Asks Mavis Ming
to Make a Sacrifice*

She awoke from another nightmare.

Mavis Ming was filled with a sense of desolation worse
than she had experienced in the past.

'Oh dear,' she murmured through her night-mask.

An impression of her dream was all that was left to her,
but she seemed to recall that it involved Mr Bloom.

'What a wicked little creature! He's frightened me more
than anything's ever frightened me before. Even Donny's tan-
trums weren't as bad. He deserves to be locked up. He deserves
it. In any other world it would be his just punishment for
doing what he has done. If Doctor Volospion hadn't stopped
him, he would have raped me, for sure. Oh, why can't I stop
thinking about what he said to me? It's all nonsense. I wish
I was braver. I can't believe he's safely out of the way. I wish
I had the nerve to go and see for myself. It would make me feel
so much better.'

She sank into her many pillows, pulling the sheets over
her eyes. 'I know what those energy cages are like. It's the
same sort I was in when I first arrived. He'll never get out.
And I can't go to see him. That ridiculous flattery. And Doctor
Volospion doesn't help by telling me all the time that he
thinks Bloom's love is "genuine", whatever *that* means. Oh,
it's worse now. It is. Why couldn't Doctor Volospion have
made him go away? Keeping him here is *torture*!'

Doctor Volospion had even suggested, earlier, that it would
be charitable if she went to his cage to 'comfort' him.

'Repulsive little runt!' She pushed her pink silky sheets

and turned up the lamp (already fairly bright) whose stand was in the shape of a flesh-coloured nymph rising naked from the powder-blue petals of an open rose. 'I do wish Doctor Volospion would let me have a power ring of my own. It would make everything much easier. Everyone else has them. Lots of time travellers do.' She crossed the soft pale yellow carpet to her gilded Empire-style dressing-table to look at her face in the mirror.

'Oh, I look *awful*! That dreadful creature.'

She sighed. She often had trouble sleeping, for she was very highly-strung, but this was much worse. For all their extravagant entertainments, their parties where the world was moulded to their whims, what they really needed, thought Mavis, was a decent TV network. TV would be just the answer to her problems right now.

'Perhaps Doctor Volospion could find something for me in one of those old cities,' she mused. 'I'll ask him. Not that he seems to be doing me many favours, these days. How long's he had the Fireclown now? A couple of weeks? And spending all his time down there. Maybe he loves Bloom and that's what it's all about.' She laughed, but immediately became miserable again.

'Oh, Mavis. Why is it always you? The world just isn't on your side.' She gave one of her funny little crooked smiles, very similar to those she had seen Barbara Stanwyck giving in those beautiful old movies.

'If only I could have gone *back* in time, to the twentieth century, even, where the sort of clothes and lifestyle they had were so *graceful*. They had simpler lives, then. Oh, I know they must have had their problems, but how I wish I could be there now! It's what I was looking forward to, when they elected me to be the first person to try out the time machine. Of course, it was proof of how popular I was with the other guys at the department. Everyone agreed unanimously that I should be the first to go. It was a great honour.'

Apparently, this thought did not succeed in lifting her spirits. She raised a hand to her head.

'Oh, oh—here comes the headache! Poor old Mavis!'

She began to pad back towards the big circular bed. But the thought of a continuance of those dreams, even though she had pushed them right out of her mind, stopped her. It had been Doctor Volospion's suggestion that she continue to lead the sort of life she had been used to—with regular periods of darkness and daylight and a corresponding need to sleep and eat, even though he could easily have changed all that for her.

To be fair to him, she thought, he tended to follow a similar routine himself, ever since he had heard that Lord Jagged of Canaria had adopted this ancient affectation. If she had a power ring or an air car at her disposal (again she was completely reliant on Volospion's good graces) she would have left the palace and gone to find some fun, something to take her mind off things. She looked at her Winnie-the-Pooh clock— another three hours before the palace would be properly activated. Until then she would not even be able to get a snack with which to console herself.

'I'm not much better off than that little creep down there,' she said. 'Oh, Mavis, what sort of a state have they got you into!'

A tap, now, at the door.

Grateful for the interruption Mavis pulled on her fluffy blue dressing robe. 'Come in!'

Doctor Volospion, a satanic Hamlet in black and white doublet and hose, entered her room. 'You are not sleeping, Miss Ming? I heard your voice as I passed ...'

Hope revealed itself in her eyes. 'I've got a bit of a headache, Doctor.' He could normally cure her headaches. Her mood improved. She became eager, anxious to win his approval. 'Silly little Mavis is having nightmares again.'

'You are unhappy?'

'Oh, no! In this lovely room? In your lovely palace? It's everything a little girl dreams about. It's just that awful Mr Bloom. Ever since ...'

'I see.' The saturnine features showed enlightenment. 'You are still afraid. He can never escape, Miss Ming. He has tried, but I assure you my powers are far greater than his. He

134

becomes tiresome, but he is no threat.'

'You'll let him go, then?'

'If I could be sure that he would leave the planet, for he fails to be as entertaining as I had hoped. And if he would give me that Grail of his, from which his power, I am now certain, derives. But he refuses.'

'You could take it now, couldn't you?'

'Not from him. Not from his ship. The screen is still impenetrable. No, you are our only hope.'

'Me?'

'He would not have allowed himself to be trapped at all, if it had not been for you.' Doctor Volospion sighed deeply. 'Well, I have just returned from visiting him again. I have offered him his liberty in return for that one piece of property, but he fobs me off with arguments that are typically specious, with vague talk of Faith and Trust—you have heard his babble.'

Mavis murmured sympathetically. 'I've never seen you so cast down, Doctor Volospion. You never know with some people, do you? He's best locked up for his own good. He's a sort of cripple, isn't he? You know what some cripples are like. You can't blame them. It's the frustration. It's all bottled up in them. It turns them into sex maniacs.'

'To do him justice, Miss Ming, his interest seems only in you. I have offered him many women, both real and artificial, from the menageries. Many of them are very beautiful, but he insists that none of them has your "soul", your—um—true beauty.'

'Really?' She was sceptical, still. 'He's insane. A lot of men are like that. That's one of the reasons I gave them up. At least with a lady you know where you are on that score. And Mr Bloom has got about as much sex-appeal as a seagull—less! Did you ever hear of a really sweet old book called *Jonathan* . . .'

'Your headache is better, Miss Ming?'

'Why, yes.' She touched her hair. 'It's almost gone. Did you . . .?'

Doctor Volospion drew his own brows together and traced

beringed fingers across the creases. 'You do not give yourself enough credit, Miss Ming ...'

She smiled. 'That's what Betty was always telling me when I used to feel low. But poor old Mavis ...'

'He demands that you see him. He speaks of nothing else.'

'Oh!' She paused. She shook her head. 'No, I couldn't, really. As it is, I haven't had a good night's sleep since the day he arrived.'

'Of course, I understand.'

Miss Ming was touched by Doctor Volospion's uncharacteristic sadness. He seemed to have none of his usual confidence. She moved closer to him.

'Don't worry, Doctor Volospion. Maybe it would be best if you tried to forget about him.'

'I need the Grail. I am obsessed with it. And I cannot rid myself of the notion that, somehow, *he* is tricking *me*.'

'Impossible. You're far too clever. Why is this Grail so important to you?'

Doctor Volospion withdrew from her.

'I'm sorry,' she said. 'I didn't mean to pry.'

'Only you can help me, Miss Ming.'

The apparent pleading in his voice moved her to heights of sympathy. 'Oh ...'

'You could convince him, I think, where I could not.'

She was relenting, against all her instincts. 'Well, if I saw him for a few moments ... And it might help me, too—to lay the ghost, if you know what I mean.'

His voice was low. 'I should be very grateful to you, Miss Ming. Perhaps we should go immediately.'

She hesitated. Then she patted his arm. 'Oh, all right. Give me a few minutes to get dressed.'

With a deep bow, Doctor Volospion left the room.

Miss Ming began to consider her clothes. On the one hand, she thought, some sort of sexless boiler suit would be best, to dampen Mr Bloom's ardour as much as possible. Another impulse was to put on her very sexiest clothes, to feed her vanity. In the end she compromised, donning a flowery mou-mou which, she thought, disguised her plumpness.

Courageously, she went to join Doctor Volospion, who awaited her in the corridor. Together they made their way to the menagerie.

As they descended flights of stone stairs she observed: 'Surprisingly, I'm feeling quite light-headed. Almost gay!'

They passed through the tiered rows of his many devotional trophies, past the bones and the sticks and the bits of cloth, the cauldrons, idols, masks and weapons, the crowns and the boxes, the scrolls, tablets and books, the prayer-wheels and crystals and ju-jus, until they reached the door of the first section of the menagerie, the Jewish House.

'I had thought of putting him in here,' Doctor Volospion told her as they passed by the inmates, who ranted, wailed, chanted, tore their clothing or merely turned aside as they passed, 'but finally I decided on the Non-Sectarian Prophet House.'

'I hadn't realised your collection was so big. I've never seen it all, as you know.' Miss Ming made conversation as best she could. Evidently, the place still disturbed her.

'It grows almost without one realising it,' said Doctor Volospion. 'I suppose, because so many people of a messianic disposition take an interest in the future, we are bound to get more than our fair share of prophets, anxious to discover if their particular version of the millenium has come about. Because they are frequently disappointed, many are glad of the refuge I offer.'

They went through another door.

'Martyrdom, it would seem, is the next best thing to affirmation,' he said.

They passed through a score of different Houses until, finally, they came to the Fireclown's habitat. It was designed to resemble a desert, scorched by a permanently blazing sun.

'He refused,' whispered Doctor Volospion, as they approached, 'to tell me what sort of environment he favoured, so I chose this one. It is the most popular with my prophets, as you'll have noted.'

Emmanuel Bloom, in his clown's costume, sat on a rock in the centre of his energy cage. His greasepaint seemed to have run a little, as if he had been weeping, but he did not seem in particularly low spirits now. He had not, it appeared, noticed them. He was reciting poetry to himself.

'... Took shape and were unfolded like as flowers.
   'And I beheld the hours
'As maidens, and the days as labouring men,
   'And the soft nights again
'As wearied women to their own souls wed,
   'And eyes as the dead.
'And over these living, and them that died,
   'From one to the other side
'A lordlier light than comes of earth or air
   'Made the world's future fair.
'A woman like to love in face, but not
   'A thing of transient lot—
'And like to hope, but having hold on truth—
   'And like to joy or youth,
'Save that upon the rock her feet were set—
   'And like what men forget,
'Faith, innocence, high thought, laborious peace—'

He had seen her. His great blue eyes blinked. His stiff little body began to rise. His bird-like, fluting voice took on a different tone.

'And yet like none of these ...' He put an awkward finger to his small mouth. He put his painted head on one side.

Mavis Ming cleared her throat. Doctor Volospion's hand forced her further towards the cage.

The Fireclown spoke first. 'So Guinevere comes at last to her Lancelot—or is it Kundry, come to call me Parsival? Sorceress, you have incarcerated me. Tell your servant to release me so that, in turn, I may free you from the evil that holds you with stronger bonds than any that chain me!'

Miss Ming's smile was insincere. 'Why don't you talk properly, Mr Bloom? This is childish. Anyway, you know he's not my servant.' She was very pale.

Mr Bloom crossed the stretch of sand until he was as close

to her as the cage permitted. 'He is not your master, you may be sure of that, this imitation Klingsor!'

'I haven't the faintest idea what you're talking about.' Her voice was shaking.

He pressed his tiny body against the energy screen. 'I must be free,' he said. 'There is no mission for me here, now, at the End of Time. I must continue my quest, perhaps into another Universe where Faith may yet flourish.'

Doctor Volospion came forward. 'I have brought Miss Ming, as you have so constantly demanded. You have talked to her. Now, if you will give up the Grail to me ...'

Mr Bloom's manner became agitated. 'I have explained to you, demi-demon, that you could not keep it, even if, by some means, I *could* transfer it to you. Only the pure in spirit are entitled to its trust. If I agreed to your bargain I should lose the Grail myself, for ever. Neither would gain!'

'I find your objections without foundation.' Doctor Volospion was unruffled by the Fireclown's anger. 'What you believe, Mr Bloom, is one thing. The truth, however, is quite another! Faith dies, but the objects of faith do not, as you saw in my museum.'

'These things have no value without Faith!'

'They are valuable to me. That is why I collect them. I desire this Grail of yours so that I may, at least, compare it with my own.'

'You know yours to be false,' said the Fireclown. 'I can tell.'

'I shall decide which is false and which is not when I have both in my possessions. I know it is on your ship, for all that you deny it.'

'It is not. It manifests itself at certain times.'

Doctor Volospion allowed his own ill-temper to show. 'Miss Ming ...'

'Please let him have it, Mr Bloom,' said Mavis Ming in her best wheedling voice. 'He'll let you go if you do.'

The Fireclown was amused. 'I can leave whenever I please. But I gave my word on two matters. I said that I would not take you by force and that I would take you with me when I left.'

'Your boasts are shown to be empty, sir,' said Doctor Volospion. He laid the flat of his hand against the energy screen. 'There.'

Mr Bloom ran his hand through his auburn mop, continuing to speak to Miss Ming. 'You demean yourself, woman, when you aid this wretch, when you adopt that idiotic tone of voice.'

'Well!' It was possible to observe that Miss Ming's legs were shaking. 'I'm not staying here, not even for you, Doctor Volospion! It's too much. I can stand a lot of things, but not this.'

'Be silent!' The Fireclown's voice was low and firm. 'Listen to your soul. It will tell you what I tell you.'

'Miss Ming!' Seeing that she prepared to flee, Doctor Volospion seized her arm. 'For my sake do not give up. If I have that Grail ...'

'You may see the Grail, beautiful Mavis, when I have redeemed you,' murmured the Fireclown. 'But it shall always be denied to such as he! Come with me and I shall let you witness more than Mystery.'

She panicked. 'Oh, Christ!' She was unable to control herself as she sensed the terrible pressure coming from both sides. She tried to free herself from Doctor Volospion's restraining hand. 'I can't take any more. I can't!'

'Miss Ming!' fiercely croaked a desperate Volospion. 'You promised to help.'

'Come with me!' cried the Fireclown.

She still struggled, trying to prise his grip away from the sleeve of her mou-mou. 'You can both do what you like. I don't want any part of it.'

Hysteria ruled now. She scratched Doctor Volospion's hand so that at last he released her. She ran away from them. She ran crazily between the cages of roaring, screaming, moaning prophets. 'Leave me alone! Leave me alone!'

And then, just before a door shut her from their view:

'I'm sorry! I'm sorry!'

CHAPTER FOURTEEN

*In which Miss Mavis Ming is Given an Opportunity
to Win the Forgiveness of
her Protector*

When Mavis Ming next awoke, finding herself in the soft
pink security of her own bed, whence she had fled in terror
after scratching Doctor Volospion, she was surprised by how
refreshed she felt, how confident. Even the threat of Doctor
Volospion's anger, which she feared almost as much as the
Fireclown's love, failed to thrill her.

'What can he do, after all?' she asked herself. She still
wore the mou-mou. She looked at the ripped sleeve, and she
inspected the bruise on her arm. She doubted if the scratch
she had given Doctor Volospion was any worse than the
bruise he had given her, but she also recalled that, in her
experience, men had a different way of looking at these things.

'Why do I feel so good? Because of a fight?' She was almost buoyant. 'Maybe because it's over. I tried to please him.
I really tried. But he's got a way of double-binding a girl like
nobody else. I guess little Mavis will have to find a new
berth.'

She removed the mou-mou and went to take a shower.
'Well, it was high time for a change. And I'm not much gone
on sharing the same roof with that mad midget downstairs.'

The shower was refreshing.

'I'm going to go out. I'm going to visit a few people. Now,'
elbow on palm of hand, finger-tip to chin, 'who shall I visit
first?'

She reviewed her acquaintances, wondering who would be
most sympathetic. Who would welcome her.

And then, of a sudden, depression swept back. It caught her so unexpectedly that she had to sit down on the edge of the unmade bed, dropping her towel to the floor. 'Oh, Christ! Oh, Christ! What in hell's wrong with you, Mavis?'

A knock on her door interrupted the catharsis before it had properly got under way.

'Yes?'

'Miss Ming?' It was, of course, Doctor Volospion.

'This is it, Mavis.' She pulled herself together. She put on a robe. 'Time for the tongue-lashing. Well. I'll tell him I'm leaving. He'll be glad of that.' She raised her voice. 'Come in!'

But he was smiling when he entered.

She looked at him in nervous astonishment.

He was dressed in robes of scarlet and green. There was a tight-fitting dark green hood on his head, emphasising the sharpness of his features.

'You are well, Miss Ming?' As he spoke he drew on dark green gloves.

'Better than I thought. I wanted to . . .'

'I came to apologise,' he said.

She had glanced at his hand before the glove went on. There was, of course, no sign of her scratch.

'Oh,' she said. She was taken aback.

'If I had realised exactly how badly that Mr Bloom affected you, I would never have subjected you to the ordeal,' he said.

'Well, you weren't to know.' She bit her lip, as if she sensed her determination dissipating already.

'The fault was wholly mine.' He had all his old authority. It comforted her.

'I lost my cool, I guess.' Her voice shook. 'I'm sorry about your hand.'

'I deserved worse.'

His voice was warm and, as always, it caused her to purr. It would not have been surprising if she had arched her back and rubbed her body against him. 'That Mr Bloom, he just freaks me, Doctor Volospion. I don't know what it is. I suppose I've completely blown it for you, haven't I?'

'No, no,' he reassured her.

'You talked? After I'd gone?'

'Somewhat. He remains quite adamant.'

'He won't give you the Grail?'

'Unfortunately, not . . .'

'It *was* my fault. I'm *really* sorry.' She responded almost without any sort of consciousness, mesmerised by him.

'It grieves me. I can think of no way of obtaining it without your help.'

'You know I'd like to.' The words emerged as if another spoke them for her. 'I mean, if there's anything I can do to make up for what happened last night . . .'

'I would not put you to further embarrassment.' He turned to leave.

'Oh, no!' She paused, making an effort of will. 'I mean, I couldn't face actually seeing him again, but if there's anything else . . .'

'I can think of nothing. Good-bye, Miss Ming.'

'There must be something?'

He paused by the door, frowning. 'Well, I suppose it is possible for you to get the Grail for me.'

'How?'

'He said that he would allow you to see it, you recall?'

'I can't really remember the details of what he said. I was too frightened.'

'Quite. You see somehow he controls his ship's protective devices from where he is. After you had gone he told me again that he would let you see the Grail, but not me. I think he believes that if you see it you will realise that he is this spiritual saviour he sets himself up to be.'

'You mean I could get into the ship and find the Grail?'

'Exactly. Once I had it in my possession, I would let him go. You would be free of him.'

'But he'd suspect.'

'His infatuation blinds him.'

'I wouldn't have to see him again?' She spoke as firmly as she could. 'I won't do that, whatever else.'

'You will never be asked to go to the menagerie and, in a while, he will have left this planet.'

'It's stealing, of course,' she said.

'Call it recompense for all the damage he has done while here. Call it justice.'

'Yes. That's fair enough.'

'But no,' he looked kindly down on her. 'I ask too much of you.'

'You don't, really.' He had inspired in her a kind of eager courage. 'Let me help.'

'He has assured me that he will lower the barriers of his ship for you alone.'

'Then it's up to Mavis, isn't it?'

'If you feel you can do it, Miss Ming, I would show my gratitude to you in many ways when you returned with the cup.'

'It's enough to help out.' But she glanced at the power rings on his gloved fingers. 'When shall I go?' She paused. 'There won't be any danger, I suppose ...?'

'None at all. He genuinely loves you, Miss Ming. Of course, if you consider this action a betrayal of Mr Bloom ...'

'Betrayal? I didn't make any deals with him.'

His voice was rich with gratification. 'It would mean much to me, as you know. My collection is important to my happiness. If I thought that I possessed an artifact that was not authentic, well, I should never be content.'

'Rely on Mavis.' Her eyes began to shine.

'You are possessed of a great and admirable generosity,' he said.

His praise sent a pulse of well-being through her whole body.

CHAPTER FIFTEEN

---

*In which Mavis Sets off in Search of
the Holy Grail*

Doctor Volospion had made no alterations to his force-screen since the Fireclown had passed beyond it. Mavis Ming moved through the eternal twilight of the castle's grounds, towards the dark and ragged hole in the wall of ice. On the other side of the hole she could see the brilliant scarlet of Emmanuel Bloom's ship.

Gingerly, she stepped through the gap, sensitive to the stillness and silence of her surroundings. She wished that Doctor Volospion had been able to accompany her, at least this far, but he was wary, he had told her, of the Fireclown suspecting treachery. If Bloom detected another presence, it was likely that he would immediately restore his ship's defences.

The teardrop-shaped ship was a red silhouette against a background of dark trees. Its airlock remained open, its ramp was down. She paused as she looked up at it.

It was impossible from where she stood to see anything of the ship's interior, but she could smell a warm mustiness coming from the entrance, together with a suggestion of pale smoke. If she had not known otherwise, she might have suspected the Fireclown still inside. The ship was redolent of his presence.

She spoke aloud, to dispell the silence. 'Here goes, Mavis.'

She was wearing her blue and orange kimono over her bikini, for Doctor Volospion had warned her that it might be uncomfortably warm within the Fireclown's ship. She struggled up the pebbled surface of the ramp and hesitated again outside the entrance, peering in. It seemed to her that points of fire still flickered on the other side of the airlock's open door.

'Coo-ee!' she said.

She wet her lips. 'What manner of creature is lord of this fair castle?' She reassured herself with the language of her favourite books. 'Shall I find my handsome prince within? Or an ugly ogre ...?' She shuddered. She looked back at the battlements and towers of gloomy Castle Volospion, hoping perhaps to see her protector, but the castle seemed entirely deserted. She drew a breath and entered the airlock. It was not quite as warm as she had been led to believe.

She moved from the airlock into the true interior of the ship. She found herself pleasantly surprised by its ordinariness. It was as if firelight illuminated the large chamber, although the source of that light was mysterious.

The rosy, flickering light cast her shadow, enlarged and distorted, upon the far wall. The chamber was in disorder, as if the shock of landing had dislodged everything from its place. Boxes, parchments, books and pictures were scattered everywhere; figurines lay dented or broken upon the carpeted floor; drapes, once used to cover portholes, hung lopsidedly upon the walls, which curved inwards.

'What a lot of junk!' Her voice held more confidence. Apparently, the place had been Mr Bloom's store-room, for there was no sign of furniture.

She stumbled over crates and bales of cloth until she reached a companionway leading up to the next chamber. Doctor Volospion had told her that she would probably find the cup in the control room, which must be above. She climbed, pushed open a hatch, and found herself in a circular room which was lit very similarly to the storage chamber, but so realistically that she found herself searching for the open fireplace which seemed to be the source of the light.

Save for a faint smell of burning timber, there was no sign of a fire.

'Mavis,' she said determinedly, 'keep that imagination of yours well under control!'

This room, as she had suspected, was the Fireclown's living

quarters. It contained a good-sized bed, shelves, storage lockers, a desk, a chair and a screen whereby the occupant could check the ship's functions.

She wiped sweat from her forehead, glancing around her.

Against one wall, at the end of the bed, was a large metal ziggurat which looked as if it had once been the base for something else. Would this be where the cup was normally kept? If so, Emmanuel Bloom had hidden it and her job was going to be harder. On the wall were various pictures: some were paintings, others photographs and holographs, primarily of men in the costumes of many periods. On the wall, too, was a narrow shelf, about two feet long, apparently empty. She reached to touch it and felt something there. It was thin, like a long pencil. Curiously, she rolled the object towards her until it fell into her hand. She was surprised.

It was an old-fashioned riding crop, its tip frayed and dividing at one end; a silver head at the other. The head was beautifully made—a woman's face in what the Italians called the 'stile Liberty'. Mavis was impressed most by the look of ineffable tranquillity upon the features. The contrast between the woman's expression and the function of the whip itself disturbed Mavis so much that she replaced it hastily.

Wishing that the light were stronger, she began to search for the cup or goblet (Doctor Volospion's description had been vague). First, she looked under the bed, finding only a collection of books and manuscripts, many of them dusty.

'This whole ship could do with a good spring-clean!' She searched through the wardrobe and drawers, finding a collection of clothes to match those worn by the men whose pictures decorated the wall. This sudden intimacy with Mr Bloom's personal possessions had not only whetted her curiosity about him—his clothes, to her, were much more interesting than anything he had said—but had somehow given her a greater sympathy for him.

She began to feel unhappy about rummaging through his things; her search for the goblet became increasingly to seem like simple thievery.

Her search became more rapid as she sought to find the

Grail and leave as soon as she could. If she had not made a promise to Doctor Volospion, she would have left the ship there and then.

'You're a fool, Mavis. Everyone's told you. And do you ever listen?'

As she opened a mahogany trunk, inlaid with silver and mother-of-pearl, the lid squeaked and, at the same time, she thought she heard a faint noise from below. She paused and listened, but there was no further sound. She saw at once that the trunk contained only faded manuscripts.

Miss Ming decided to return to the store-room. The curiosity which had at first directed her energy was now dissipating, to be replaced by a familiar sense of panic.

She felt her heart-rate increase and the ship seemed to give a series of little tremors, in sympathy. She returned to the companionway and lifted the hatch. She was halfway down when the whole ship shook itself like an animal, roared, as if sentient, and she was pressed back against the steps, clinging to the rail as, swaying from side to side, the ship took off.

Sweating, Miss Ming turned herself round with difficulty and began to climb back towards the living quarters where she felt she would be safer. If her throat had been less constricted, she would have screamed. The ship, she knew, was taking off under its own power. It was quite possible that she had activated it herself. Unless she could work out how to control it she would soon be adrift in the cosmos, floating through space until she died.

And she would be all alone.

It was this latter thought which terrified her most. She reached the cabin and crawled across the dusty carpet as the pressure increased, climbing on to the bed in the hope that it would cushion the acceleration effects.

The sensations she was experiencing were not dissimilar to those she had experienced on her trip through Time and, as such, did not alarm her. It was the prospect of what would become of her when the ship was beyond Earth's gravity which she could not bear to consider.

It was not, she thought, as if there were many planets left

148

in the Universe. Earth might now be the only one.

The pressure began to lift, but she remained face down upon the bed ('these sheets could do with a wash', she was thinking) even when it was obvious that the ship was travelling at last through free space.

'Oh, you've let yourself in for it this time, Mavis,' she told herself. 'You've been conned properly, my girl.'

She wondered if, for reasons of his own, Doctor Volospion had deliberately sent her into space. She knew his capacity for revenge. Had that silly tiff meant so much to him? He had beguiled her into suggesting her own trap, her own punishment, just because of a silly scratch on the hand!

'What a bastard! What bastards they all are!' And what an idiot she had made of herself! It taught you never to be sympathetic to a man. They always used it against you. 'That's Mavis all over,' she continued, 'trusting the world. And this is how the world repays you!' But there was little conviction in her tone; her self-pity was half-hearted. Actually, she realised, she was not feeling particularly bad now that there was a genuine threat to her life. All the little anxieties fled away.

Miss Ming began to roll over on the bed. At least the ship itself was comfortable enough.

'It's cosy, really.' She smiled. 'A sort of den. Just like when I was a little girl, with my own little room, and my books and dolls.' She laughed. 'I'm actually safer here than anywhere I've been since I grew up. It shouldn't be difficult to work out a way of getting back to Earth—*if* I want to go back. What's Earth got to offer, anyway, except deceit, hypocrisy and treachery?'

She swung her legs over the edge of the bed. She looked at her new home, all her new toys.

'I think it's really what I've always wanted,' she declared.

'Now you realise that I spoke the truth!' said the triumphant voice of Emmanuel Bloom from the shadows overhead.

'My God!' said Miss Ming as she realised the full extent of Doctor Volospion's deception.

CHAPTER SIXTEEN

*In which Doctor Volospion Receives the Congratulations
of his Peers and Celebrates the Acquisition
of his new Treasure*

My Lady Charlotina rose from Doctor Volospion's bed and
swiftly demolished her double (Doctor Volospion would only
make love to pairs of women) before touching a power ring
to adorn herself in white and cerise poppies. In the shadows
of the four-poster Doctor Volospion lay relishing his several
victories, a beautiful cup held in his hands. He turned the cup
round and round, running his fingers over an inscription which
he could not read, for it was in ancient English.

'You doubt none of my powers now, I hope, My Lady
Charlotina,' he said.

Her smile was slow. She knew he would have her speak
of Jagged, perhaps make a comparison, but she did not have
it in her to satisfy Volospion's curiosity. Lord Jagged was
Lord Jagged, she thought.

'I was privileged,' she said, 'to know your plan from the
start and to see it work so smoothly. I am most impressed.
First, you incarcerated Miss Ming, then you lured Mr Bloom
to your castle, then you pretended that his power was great
enough to destroy your force-field, then you captured him,
knowing that he would give anything to escape. You originally
meant to hold him, of course, as one of your collection, but
then you learned of the Grail . . .'

'So I offered Miss Ming in exchange for the Grail. Thus
he thought he took her from me without force and that she
went willingly to him—for I did not, of course, explain to Mr
Bloom that I had deceived Miss Ming.'

'So much deception! It is quite hard for me to follow!' She laughed. 'What a match! The greatest cynic of our world (with the exception of Lord Shark who does not really count) pitted against the greatest idealist in the Universe!'

'And the cynic won,' said Doctor Volospion. 'As they always do.'

'Well, a cynic *would* draw that conclusion,' she pointed out. 'I had a liking for Mr Bloom, though he was a bore.'

'As was Miss Ming.'

'Great bores, both.'

'And by one stroke I rid the world of its two most awful bores,' said Doctor Volospion, in case she had not considered this achievement with the rest.

'Exactly.'

Yawning, My Lady Charlotina drifted towards a dark window. 'You have your cup. He has his queen.'

'Exactly.'

My Lady Charlotina looked up at the featureless heavens. No stars gleamed here. Perhaps they were all extinguished. She sighed.

'My only regret,' said Doctor Volospion as he carefully laid the cup upon his pillow and straightened his body, 'is that I was not able to ask Mr Bloom the meaning of this inscription.'

'Doubtless a warning to the curious,' she said 'or an offer of eternal salvation. You know more about these things, Doctor Volospion.'

A cap appeared on his head. Robes formed. Black velvet and mink. 'Oh, yes, they are always very similar. And often disappointingly ordinary.'

'It does seem a very ordinary cup.'

'The faithful would see that as a sign of its true holiness,' he told her knowledgeably.

From outside they detected a halloo.

'It is Abu Thaleb,' she said in some animation. 'And Argonheart Po and others. Li Pao, I think, is with them. Shall you admit them?'

'Of course. They will want to see my cup.'

My Lady Charlotina and Doctor Volospion left his bedroom and went down to the hall to greet their guests.

Doctor Volospion placed the cup upon the table. The ill-functioning neon played across its bright silver.

'Beautiful!' said Abu Thaleb, without as much enthusiasm as perhaps Doctor Volospion would have wished. The Commissar of Bengal brushed feathers from his eyes. 'A fitting reward for your services to us all, Doctor Volospion.'

Argonheart Po bore a tray in his great hands. He set this, now, beside the cup. 'I am always thorough in my research,' he said, 'and hope you find this small offering appropriate.' He removed the cloth to reveal his savouries. 'That is a pemmican spear. This cross is primarily the flavour of sole à la crème. The taste of the wafers and the blood is rather more difficult to describe.'

'What an elegant notion!' Doctor Volospion took one of the savouries between finger and thumb and nibbled politely.

Li Pao asked: 'May I inspect the cup?'

'Of course.' Doctor Volospion waved a generous hand. 'You do not, by any chance, read, do you, Li Pao? Specifically, Dawn Age English.'

'Once,' said Li Pao. He studied the inscription. He shook his head. 'I am baffled.'

'A great shame.'

'Does it *do* anything,' wondered Sweet Orb Mace, moving from the shadows where he had been studying Doctor Volospion's portrait.

'I think not,' said My Lady Charlotina. 'It has done nothing yet, at any rate.'

Doctor Volospion stared at his cup somewhat wistfully. 'Ah, well,' he said, 'I fear I shall grow tired of it soon enough.'

My Lady Charlotina came to stand beside him. 'Perhaps it will fill the room with light or something,' she said encouragingly.

'We can always hope,' he said.

CHAPTER SEVENTEEN

In which Miss Mavis Ming at last Attains a State of Grace

Emmanuel Bloom swung himself from the ceiling, an awkward macaw. He no longer wore his paint and motley but was again dressed in his black velvet suit.

Mavis Ming saw that he had entered by means of a hatch. Doubtless, the control cabin of the ship was above.

'My Goddess,' said the Fireclown.

She still sat on the edge of the bed. Her voice was without emotion. 'You traded me for the cup. That's what it was all about. What a fool I am!'

'No, not you. Doctor Volospion proposed the bargain and so enabled me to keep my word to him. He demanded the cup which I kept in my ship. I gave it to him.' He strutted across the cabin and manipulated a dial. Red-gold light began to fill his living quarters. Now everything glowed and each piece of fabric, wood or metal seemed to have a life of its own.

Mavis Ming stood up and edged away from the bed. She drew her kimono about her, over her pendulous breasts, her fat stomach, her wide thighs.

'Listen,' she began. She was breathing rapidly once more. 'You can't really want me, Mr Bloom. I'm fat old Mavis. I'm ugly. I'm stupid. I'm selfish. I should be left on my own. I'm better off on my own. I know I'm always looking for company, but really it's just because I never realised ...'

He raised a stiff right arm in a gesture of impatience. 'What has any of that to do with my love for you? What does it matter if foolish Volospion thought he was killing two birds with one stone when he was actually freeing two eagles?'

'Look,' she said, 'if . . .'

'I am the Fireclown! I am Bloom, the Fireclown! I have lived the span of Man's existence. I have made Time and Space my toys. I have juggled with chronons and made the Multiverse laugh. I have mocked Reality and Reality has shrivelled to be re-born. My eyes have stared unblinking into the hearts of stars, and I have stood at the very core of the Sun and feasted on freshly created photons. I am Bloom, Eternally Blooming Bloom. Bloom the Phoenix. Bloom, the Destroyer of Darkness. These eyes, these large bulging eyes of mine, do you think they cannot see into souls as easily as they see into suns? Can they not detect an aura of pain that disguises the true centre of a being as smoke hides fire? That is why I choose to make you wise, to enslave you so that you may know true freedom.'

Miss Ming forced herself to speak. 'This is kidnapping and kidnapping is kidnapping whatever you prefer to call it . . .'

He ignored her.

'Of all the beings on that wasteland planet, you were one of the few who still lived. Oh, you lived as a frightened rodent lives, your spirit perverted, your mind enshelled with cynicism, refusing for a moment to look upon Reality for fear that it would detect you and devour you, like a wakened lion. Yet when Reality occasionally impinged and could not be escaped, how did you respond?'

'Look,' she said, 'you've got no right . . .'

'Right? I have every right! I am Bloom! You are my Bride, my Consort, my Queen, my Goddess. There is no woman deserves the honour more!'

'Oh, Christ!' she said. 'Please let me go. Please, I can't give you anything. I can't understand you. I can't love you.' She began to cry. 'I've never loved anyone! No one but myself.'

His voice was gentle. He took a few jerky steps closer to her. 'You lie, Mavis Ming. You do not love yourself.'

'Donny said I did. They all said I did, sooner or later.'

'If you loved yourself,' he told her, 'you would love me.'

Her voice shook. 'That's good . . .'

154

To Mavis Ming's own ears her words were without resonance of any kind. The collection of platitudes with which she had always responded to; the borrowed ironies, the barren tropes with which, instinctively, she had encumbered herself in order to placate a world she had seen as essentially malevolent, all were at once revealed as the meaningless things they were, with the result that an appalling self-consciousness, worse than anything she had suffered in the past, swept over her and every phrase she had ever uttered seemed to ring in her ears for what it had been: A mew of pain, a whimper of frustration, a cry for attention, a groan of hunger.

'Oh ...'

She became incapable of speech. She could only stare at him, backing around the wall as he came, half-strutting, half-hopping, towards her, his head on one side, an appalling amusement in his unwinking, protruberant eyes, until her escape was blocked by a heavy wardrobe.

She became incapable of movement. She watched as he reached a twitching hand towards her face; the hand was firm and gentle as it touched her and its warmth made her realise how cold, how clammy, her own skin felt. She was close to collapse, only supported by the wall of the ship.

'The Earth is far behind us now,' he said. 'We shall never return. It does not deserve us.' He pointed to the bed. 'Go there. Remove your clothes.'

She gasped at him, trying to make him understand that she could not walk. She did not care, now, what his intentions were, but she was too exhausted to obey him.

'Tired ...' she said at last.

He shook his head. 'No. You shall not escape by that route, madam.' He spoke kindly. 'Come.'

The high-pitched ridiculous voice carried greater authority than any she had heard before. She began to walk towards the bed. She stood looking down at the sheets; the light made these, too, seem vibrant with life of their own. She felt his little claw-like hands pull the kimono from her shoulders, undo the tie, removing the garment entirely.

She felt him break the fastening on her bikini top so that

155

her breasts hung even lower on her body. She felt no revulsion, nothing sexual at all, as his fingers pushed the bikini bottom over her hips and down her legs. And yet she was more aware of her nakedness than she had ever been, seeing the fatness, the pale flesh, without any emotion at all, remarking its poor condition as if it did not belong to her.

'Fat ...' she murmured.

His voice was distant. 'It is of no importance, this body. Besides, it shall not be fat for very long.'

She began to anticipate his rape of her, wondering if, when he began, she would feel anything. He ordered her to lie face down upon the bed. She obeyed. She heard him move away, then. Perhaps he was undressing. She turned to look, but he was still in his tattered velvet suit, taking something from a shelf. She saw that he held the whip in his hand, the one she had discovered earlier.

She tried to feel afraid, because she knew that she should feel fear, but fear would not come. She continued to look up at him, over her shoulder, as he returned. Still her body made no response. This was quite unlike her fantasies of flagellation. What happened now neither excited her imagination nor her body. She wished that she could feel something, even terror. Instead she was possessed by a calmness, a sense of inevitability, unlike anything she had known.

'Now,' she heard him say, 'I shall bring your blood into the light. And with it shall come the devils that inhabit it, to be withered as weeds in the sun. And when I have finished you will know Rebirth, Freedom, Dominion over the Multiverse, and more.'

Was it a mark of her own insanity that she could detect no insanity in his words?

The whip fell upon her flesh. It struck her buttocks and the pain stole her breath. She did not scream, but she gasped.

It struck again, just below the first place, and she thought his flames lashed her. Her whole body jerked, trying to escape, but a firm hand held her down again, and again the whip fell.

She did not scream, but she groaned as she drew in her breath. The next stroke was upon her thighs, the next behind her knees, and his hands were cruel now as she struggled. He held her by the back of the neck; he gripped her by the shoulder, by the loose flesh of her waist, and each time he gripped her she knew fresh pain.

Mavis Ming believed at last that it was Emmanuel Bloom's intention to flay her alive, to tear every piece of skin from her body. He held her lips, her ears, her breasts, her vagina, the tender parts of her inner thighs, and every touch was fire.

She screamed, she blubbered for him to stop, she could not believe that he, any more than she, was any longer in control of what was happening. And yet the whip fell with a regularity which denied her even this consolation, until, at length, her whole body burned and she lay still, consumed.

Slowly, the fire faded from this peak of intensity and it seemed to her that, again, her body and her mind were united; this unity was new.

Emmanuel Bloom said nothing. She heard him cross the chamber to replace the whip. She began to breathe with deep regularity, as if she slept. Her consciousness of her body produced an indefinable emotion in her. She moved her head to look at him and the movement was painful.

'I feel . . .' Her voice was soft.

He stood with his arms stiffly at his sides. His head was cocked, his expression was tender and expectant.

She could find no word.

'It is your pride,' he said.

He reached to caress her face.

'I love you,' he said.

'I love you.' She began to weep.

He made her rise and look at her body in the oval mirror he revealed. It seemed that her skin was a lattice of long, red bruises; she could see where he had gripped her shoulders and her breasts. The pain was hard to tolerate without making at least a whisper of sound, but she controlled herself.

'Will you do this again?' It was almost a request.

He shook his little head.

She walked back to the bed. Her back, though lacerated, was straight. She had never walked in that way before, with

157

dignity. She sat down. 'Why did you do it?'

'In this manner? Perhaps because I lack patience. It is one of my characteristics. It was quick.' He laughed. 'Why do it to you, at all? Because I love you. Because I wished to reveal to you the woman that you are, the individual that you are. I had to destroy the shell.'

'It won't fade, this feeling?'

'Only the scars will go. It is within you to retain the rest. Will you be my wife?'

She smiled. 'Yes.'

'Well, then, this had been a satisfactory expedition, after all. Better, really, than I expected. Oh, what leaping delights we shall share, what wonders I can show you! No woman could desire more than to be the consort of Bloom, the Good Soldier, the Champion Eternal, the Master of the Multiverse!'

'And my master, too.'

'As you are my mistress, Mavis Ming.' He fell with a peculiar, spastic jerk, on his knees beside her. 'For Eternity. Will you stay? I can return you within an hour or two.'

'I will stay,' she said. 'Yet you gave up so much for me. That cup. It was your honour?'

He looked shamefaced. 'He asked for the cup I kept in my ship. I could not give him the Holy Grail, for it is not mine to give. I gave him something almost as dear to me, however. If Doctor Volospion ever deciphers the inscription on the cup, he will discover that it was awarded, in 1980, to Leonard Bloom, by the Union of Master Bakers, for the best matzo bread of the Annual Bakery Show, Whitechapel, London. He was a very good baker, my father. I loved him. I had kept his cup in all my journeys back and forth through the Time-streams and it was the most valuable thing I possessed.'

'So you do not have the Grail.' She smiled. 'It was all part of your plan—pretending to own it, pretending to be powerless—you tricked Doctor Volospion completely.'

'And he tricked me. Both are satisfied, for it is unlikely he shall ever know the extent of my trickery and doubtless considers himself a fine fellow now! All are satisfied!'

'And now . . .?' she began.

158

'And now,' he said, 'I'll leave you. I must set my controls. You shall see all that is left of this Universe and then, through the centre of the brightest star, into the greater vastness of the Multiverse beyond! There we shall find others to inspire and if we find no life at all, upon our wanderings, it is within our power to create it, for I am the Fireclown. I am the Voice of the Sun! Aha! Look! It has come to you, too. This, my love, is Grace. This is our reward!'

The cabin was filled suddenly by brilliant golden light, apparently having as its source a beam which entered through the very shell of the spaceship, falling directly upon the ziggurat at the end of the bed.

A smell, like sweet spring flowers after the rain, filled the cabin, and then a crystal cup, brimming with scarlet liquid, appeared at the top of the ziggurat.

Scarlet rays spread from a hundred points in the crystal, almost blinding her, and, although Mavis Ming could hear nothing, she received an impression of sonorous, delicate music. She could not help herself as she lifted her aching body from the bed to the floor and knelt, staring into the goblet in awe.

From behind her the Fireclown chuckled and he knelt beside her, taking her hand.

'We are married now,' he said, 'before the Holy Grail. Married individually and together. And this is our Trust which shall be taken from us should we ever commit the sin of accidia. Here is proof of all my claims. Here is Hope. And should we ever cease to forget our purpose, should we ever fall into that sin of inertia, should we lose, for more than a moment, our Faith in our high resolve, the Grail will leave us and shall vanish forever from the sight of Man, for I am Bloom, the Last Pure Knight, and you are the Pure Lady, chastised and chaste, who shall share these Mysteries with me.'

She began: 'It is too much. I am not capable ...' But then she lifted her head and she smiled, staring into the very heart of the goblet. 'Very well.'

'Look,' he said, as the vision began to fade, 'your wounds have vanished.'

Wyndham Books are obtainable from many booksellers and newsagents. If you have any difficulty please send purchase price plus postage on the scale below to:

Wyndham Cash Sales
P.O. Box 11
Falmouth
Cornwall
OR
Star Book Service,
G.P.O. Box 29,
Douglas,
Isle of Man,
British Isles.

While every effort is made to keep prices low, it is sometimes necessary to increase prices at short notice. Wyndham Books reserve the right to show new retail prices on covers which may differ from those advertised in the text or elsewhere.

Postage and Packing Rate

UK: 30p for the first book, plus 15p per copy for each additional book ordered to a maximum charge of £1.29. **BFPO and Eire:** 30p for the first book, plus 15p per copy for the next 6 books and thereafter 6p per book. **Overseas:** 50p for the first book and 15p per copy for each additional book.

These charges are subject to Post Office charge fluctuations.